KT-224-471

THE CASE OF
THE BLONDE BONANZA

CONDITIONS OF SALE

ERLE STANLEY GARDNER

THE CASE OF
THE BLONDE BONANZA

PAN BOOKS LTD · LONDON

First published in Great Britain 1967
by William Heinemann Ltd.
This edition published 1971 by Pan Books Ltd,
33 Tothill Street, London, S.W.1

ISBN 0 330 02616 X

Printed in Great Britain by
Richard Clay (The Chaucer Press), Ltd., Bungay, Suffolk

FOREWORD

FROM time to time, paying tribute to outstanding leaders in the field of legal medicine, I have dedicated my books by appropriate forewords.

This book, however, is not dedicated to one individual but to a group of men.

As one who has had much to do with crime and with the trial of criminal cases, I have learned to appreciate the value of scientific investigation and of the impartial devotion to truth which characterizes the true expert.

The professional witness, who uses his technical qualifications as a springboard by which he can inject himself into a partisan position in a legal controversy, is an old-fashioned carry-over from a bygone day.

The modern expert witness regards the facts with scientific objectivity. He states the reasons for his opinions with concise logic and is the first to admit any fact which may be opposed to his opinion or which may seem to be opposed to it.

I have watched the American Academy of Forensic Sciences grow from an idea in the brain of my friend, the late Dr R. B. H. Gradwohl, to its present position of dignified power.

It is my hope that the public will learn to appreciate the importance of legal medicine, of the scientific methods of crime detection, and will learn to distrust the old-fashioned witness who testifies under the guise of an expert but is actually a professional partisan.

The scientific witness of today is interested only in finding the truth. He recites the facts as they exist, his opinion is impartial, and his voice unpartisan.

And because the American Academy of Forensic Sciences has done so much to bring all this about, I respectfully dedicate this book to:

THE AMERICAN ACADEMY OF FORENSIC SCIENCES.

Erle Stanley Gardner

THE CASE OF
THE BLONDE BONANZA

CHAPTER 1

BECAUSE DELLA STREET, Perry Mason's confidential secretary, was spending a two-week vacation with an aunt who lived at Bolero Beach, the lawyer, having consulted with a client in San Diego, drove by on the way home. Since it was Saturday, and a beautiful day, a little persuasion on Della Street's part, plus a dinner invitation from Aunt Mae, caused the lawyer to stop over at the Bolero Hotel.

'Moreover,' Della Street had pointed out, 'you can then drive me back on Monday morning.'

'Is this a pitch to get a ride back,' Mason asked, 'or a scheme on the part of you and Mae to get me to take a vacation?'

'Both,' she retorted. 'Any lawyer who gets so busy he regards a Saturday afternoon and a Sunday as being a vacation needs to be taken in hand. Aunt Mae has promised one of her chicken and dumpling dinners, the beach will be thronged with bathing beauties, and I have, moreover, a mystery.'

'You won't need the mystery,' Mason said. 'Surf, sand, sunshine, bathing beauties, and one of Mae's chicken-dumpling dinners make the law business seem drab and uninviting, the air of the office stale, and the perusal of law books a chore. I'll stay over.'

'Then,' she said, her eyes twinkling, 'you're not interested in the mystery.'

'I didn't say that,' Mason said. 'I said you had already established the proper inducement. The mystery is the frosting on the cake – not essential but delightful.'

'Put on your trunks and meet me on the beach in half an hour,' she said, 'and I'll introduce you to the mystery.'

'It's animate?'

'It's animate.'

'Two legs or four?'

'Two – and wait until you see them.'

'I'll be there in twenty minutes,' Mason promised, and actually made it in eighteen.

He found Della Street stretched out on the sand under the shade of a beach umbrella.

'And now?' he asked, surveying her sun-tanned figure approvingly.

'She should be along any minute now,' Della Street said. 'It's almost noon ... Are you hungry?'

'Ravenous,' he said, 'but in view of Mae's promise of chicken and dumplings I want to restrain my appetite for the time being.'

'I'm afraid,' she said, 'you're going to *have* to eat something— Wait a minute, here she comes now.'

Della Street indicated a curvaceous blonde walking slowly down the strip of wet sand at the margin of the waves.

'See it?' she asked.

'Every visible inch of it,' Mason said.

'Did I misjudge the legs?'

'Second most beautiful pair on the beach. I presume the mystery is, why does she always walk alone?'

'That's only one of the mysteries. Would you like to leave our things here and follow her?'

'Are they safe?'

'It's a private beach and *I* haven't had any trouble. Terry-cloth robes, sandals, and reading material seem to remain in place.'

'Let's go,' Mason said.

'The young woman in question,' Della Street said, 'is wending her way to the lunch room.'

'And we follow?'

'We follow. It's a snack bar and open-air lunch room for bathers. You can get very good food.'

'And how do we pay for it?' Mason asked, looking down at his bathing trunks.

'If you're registered at the hotel, you sign a chit. If you're not registered, but are a member of the beach club, you can also sign.'

'You promised to *introduce* me to the mystery,' Mason said, as they moved towards the lunch room.

'Notice,' she said, 'that I promised to introduce you to the mystery – not to the young woman.'

'There's a distinction?'

'Very much so. Like that between the *corpus delicti* and the corpse. As you have pointed out so many times, the average individual thinks that the *corpus delicti* in a murder case is the corpse. Actually, the expression, if I remember your statements correctly, relates to the body of the *crime* rather than the body of the *victim*.'

'And so,' Mason said, 'I take it I am introduced only to the mystery and not to the body to which the mystery pertains.'

'From this point on,' Della Street said, as they entered the lunch room, 'you're on your own. However, I may point out that during the whole ten days I have been watching her she has remained unescorted. This is indicative of the fact she is not easy.'

'And of what does the mystery consist?' Mason asked.

'What do you think of her figure?'

'I believe the expression,' Mason said, 'is well-stacked.'

'You would gather that perhaps she was fighting a weight problem?'

'One would say that weight and whistles were her two major problems in life.'

'All right,' Della Street said, 'she's seated in that booth over there. If you'll sit in this one, you can look across and see what she orders. You won't believe it,' she warned.

Mason and Della Street ordered toasted baked ham sandwiches and coffee, settled back on the waterproof cushions, and, after a few minutes' wait, saw the voluptuous blonde in the booth across the way being served with what seemed to be a glass of milk.

'That certainly seems abstemious enough,' Mason said.

'For your information,' Della Street said, 'that is a glass of half milk and half cream. I bribed the information from the waitress – and you haven't seen anything yet.'

The blonde in the bathing suit slowly drank the contents of the glass. Then the waitress brought her a sizzling steak,

11

French fried potatoes, and a salad, followed by apple pie alamode and two candy bars.

'I presume the candy bars are to keep her from getting hungry until tea time,' Mason said.

'You don't know the half of it,' Della Street said. 'She'll be back here at about four o'clock for tea. She'll have a chocolate sundae and a piece of rich cake. Her tea will consist of a chocolate malted milk.'

Mason cocked a quizzical eyebrow. 'You seem to have taken an undue interest.'

'Undue!' she exclaimed. 'I'm fascinated! I told you I bribed the waitress. They're talking about it in the kitchen. The help have totalled the calories consumed each day and the result is what would be referred to in Hollywood as super-colossal.'

'It takes that to keep the figure at its proper level?' Mason asked.

'Level is not exactly the word,' she said. 'The figure is noticeably growing. But wait until she signs the chit and leaves the booth – then see what she does.'

The blonde finished with her dessert, signed the check, picked up the two candy bars, and walked towards the entrance. On the way, she detoured long enough to stand on a pair of scales which had a huge dial with a rotating hand.

Della Street said, 'That's nearly five pounds in the last eight days.'

'You've been watching?'

'I've been watching and marvelling. The girl seems to be making a desperate, deadly, determined effort to put on weight, and she's carrying plenty already.'

'How long has this been going on, Miss Sherlock Holmes?' Mason asked.

'For about two weeks, according to the waitress.'

'This information was readily volunteered?' Mason asked.

'In return for a five-dollar tip.'

Mason said musingly, 'It's a situation that's worth looking into.'

'You've certainly looked the situation over,' Della Street said, as the blonde went through the door.

'And what does she do now?' Mason asked.

'She has a beach umbrella and she lies down, dozes, and reads.'

'No exercise?'

'Oh, yes – enough exercise to give her a healthy appetite. And while your untrained masculine eye may not appreciate the fact, Mr Perry Mason, her bathing suit is being stretched to the limit. It was tight enough to begin with, and now it seems to be about to burst – in both directions.'

'You've told your Aunt Mae about this?' Mason asked.

'I discussed it with her two or three times, and Mae came down with me yesterday to see it for herself.'

'Mae doesn't know her?' Mason asked.

Della Street said thoughtfully, 'I think she does, Perry. She had a smug smile on her face. She kept her dark glasses on while we were in the booth and sat back under my umbrella. I think she was trying to keep the blonde from seeing and recognizing her.'

'But Mae didn't admit anything?'

'Nothing. She's been busy planning the details of the chicken-dumpling feed with all of the fixings.'

Mason signed the chit for their meal, said, 'There must be a gag tied in with it somewhere, some sort of publicity stunt.'

'I know,' Della Street said, 'but what in the world *could* it be?'

'She is always alone?'

'She keeps away from all of the beach wolves. And that,' Della Street announced, 'is rather difficult.'

'I take it,' Mason said, 'that you haven't been entirely successful.'

'Perhaps,' she said, 'I haven't tried quite so determinedly. However, I let everyone know I was keeping Saturday and Sunday wide open for you.'

'Evidently you felt sure you could persuade me to stay over,' Mason said.

She smiled. 'Let's put it this way, Mr Perry Mason. I felt certain that if you didn't stay over I wouldn't have a completely disastrous afternoon or a danceless evening.'

Mason said musingly, 'Apple pie alamode ... chocolate malted milk ... there simply has to be a catch in it somewhere, Della – and there's an irresistible body meeting an immovable bathing suit. Something is bound to happen.'

'We could, of course, open a branch office here at the beach.'

'I'm afraid our clients wouldn't come that far, Della.'

'Well,' Della Street predicted, 'a bathing suit can only stretch so far.'

CHAPTER 2

MAE KIRBY greeted Perry Mason affectionately. 'It seems that I almost never see you,' she said, 'and you're keeping Della on the go all the time.'

Mason said, 'I know, Mae. Time passes faster than we realize. I keep going from one case to another.'

'At breakneck speed,' she said. 'You'd better slow down. Flesh and blood can't stand that pace. Come on in. Here's someone who wants to meet you.'

Della Street stood in the doorway, smiling at Mason and then giving him a quick wink as Mae led him into the room. She said, 'Dianne Alder, this is Perry Mason.'

The young woman who was standing by the window was the same blonde whom Mason and Della Street had been watching earlier in the day.

She gave Mason her hand and a dazzling smile. 'I'm absolutely thrilled,' she said. 'This is a wonderful privilege. I've heard about you so much and read about you, and to think of actually meeting you! It was so thoughtful of Mrs Kirby to invite me over.'

Mason glanced swiftly at Della Street, received a slight shake of the head from Della, and then said, 'You flatter me, Miss Alder. The pleasure is mine.'

Dianne Alder said, 'I've seen your secretary on the beach

several times in the last week but had no idea who she was or I'd have been bold enough to introduce myself. She's beautiful enough to make everyone think she's—'

'Come, come,' Della Street interrupted. 'You're making us all too vain, Dianne.'

Mae Kirby said, 'Now we're going to have one nice dry Martini and then we're going to have dinner – chicken and dumplings.'

Dianne Alder said, 'I've heard of Mrs Kirby's chicken and dumplings. They're almost as famous as Perry Mason.'

'You're looking forward to them?' Della Street asked.

'Am I looking forward to them? I'm simply ravenous!'

Mason and Della Street exchanged glances.

It wasn't until after the cocktails and just before sitting down to dinner that Mason was able to jockey Della Street into a corner for a hurried confidential conversation.

'What is this?' he asked. 'Some sort of a trap or frame-up?'

'I don't think so,' she said. 'It was just a surprise Aunt Mae was planning for us. She knew that I was interested and evidently she's known Dianne for some time. She invited her to come over for dinner and meet you.

'Usually Aunt Mae is very considerate. She knows there are lots of people here who are dying to meet you, and when you're here for dinner she never invites anyone else. This time is the exception.'

'Found out anything?' Mason asked.

Della shook her head and was on the point of saying something when Mae said, 'Come on now, you two. You're either talking business or making love, and you shouldn't do either on an empty stomach. Come on in here and sit down. You sit there, Perry, and Della, you sit over here. Dianne can sit next to me.'

Thirty minutes later when they had finished with their hot mince pie and coffee, Della Street said, 'Well, it was wonderful, Aunt Mae, but I'm afraid I've put on a pound and a half.'

'So have I – at least I hope I have,' Dianne said.

Mason raised his eyebrows.

There was silence for a moment and then Della Street said, 'You *hope* you have?'

'Yes, I'm trying to gain weight.'

Della Street glanced at the front of the girl's dress and Dianne laughed somewhat awkwardly. 'It's something I can't discuss,' she said. 'I know how you feel. You think I don't need it, but actually I . . . well, I have to put on another four pounds.'

'What are you going to do,' Della Street asked, 'take up wrestling? – No, no, I didn't mean it that way, Dianne. I just wondered, the way you said it, you sounded as though you were trying to make a definite weight.'

'But I am.'

Mason raised his brows in a silent question.

She flushed slightly and said, 'I don't know how the subject came up. I— Oh, skip it.'

'Of course,' Della Street said, 'we don't want to pry, but now you certainly have aroused our curiosity, and I know my boss well enough to know that when his curiosity is once aroused it gnaws at his consciousness like termites in a building. You'd better tell us – that is, if it isn't too confidential.'

'Well,' Dianne said, 'it's confidential in a way – that is, I'm not supposed to talk about it. But I know that Mrs Kirby can be just as close-lipped as anyone. That's one thing about her, she never does gossip – and for the rest of it, I'm talking to an attorney and his secretary.'

'Go ahead,' Della Street invited.

'Well,' Dianne said, 'the truth of the matter is I'm going to model a new style.'

'A new style?' Della Street asked, as Dianne broke off to laugh self-consciously.

'It sounds absolutely absurd,' she said, 'but I'm getting paid to put on weight and . . . well, that's all there is to it.'

'Now, wait a minute,' Della Street said. 'Let's see if I get this straight. You're being paid money to put on more weight?'

'Twelve pounds from the time I started.'

'Within a time limit?'

'Yes.'

16

'And someone is paying you for it?'

'Yes. Some designers. The— Oh, I know it sounds silly and ... I don't know how I got started on this. It— Well, anyway, some style designers feel that there has been too great a tendency to take off weight, that everyone is fighting weight and it isn't natural, and that people would be a lot happier and feel a lot better if they didn't keep so diet conscious, if they were free to eat what they wanted.

'Of course there are people who are simply fat, and my sponsors don't want that. They have been looking for some time for a young woman who is – well, as they expressed it, firmly fleshed, who could put on enough weight to wear certain styles they wanted to bring out. They're going to photograph me and put me on television. Well, that's it. I'm to be a new sort of model, start a trend.

'You know how it is in the fashion shows. Some slender model who concentrates on being willowy and svelte comes out modelling a dress. But the women who are sitting there looking at that dress are nearly all of them twenty to thirty pounds heavier than the model.

'My sponsors have had me examined by a physician and they feel that I can keep my waist measurement and my carriage and still put on twelve to fifteen pounds and – well, they're going to try and make curves stylish ... Oh, why did I get started on this?'

Dianne suddenly covered her scarlet face with her hands and said, 'I feel so horribly self-conscious.'

'Not at all,' Mason said, 'you interest me a lot. I think there's a good deal to this. You mentioned your sponsors, some style company?'

'Frankly,' she said, 'I don't know who the sponsors are. I'm dealing through an agency ... and I'm under contract not to discuss what I'm doing with anyone.'

'I see,' Mason said thoughtfully.

'Are you putting weight on?' Della Street asked.

'Heavens, yes! I've had to count calories for the last five years and now I'm just revelling in having everything I want. Now I've built up my appetite to a point where I just can't resist food. I'm going to make the weight all right but the hard

17

part is whether I can shut off the supply of food when I've made the weight. I'm afraid I'm going to overshoot the mark.'

Mason said, 'You certainly have the figure to make women curve-conscious and sell clothes.'

'Well, of course,' she said, 'that's what's at the back of it. They want to sell clothes. They feel that the average woman is simply sick and tired of starving herself and that I can make – that is, that *they* can make a new trend in styles if they can find the right model.'

'I think they've found her,' Mason said. And raising his coffee cup, smiled at the highly embarrassed Dianne Alder and said, 'Here's to success!'

Fifteen minutes later, however, when Mason was able to get Della Street to one side, he said, 'Della, there's something terribly fishy about this whole business with Dianne Alder. She says she has a contract. Apparently it's a written contract. She seems to be a very nice girl. I would dislike very much to see her victimized. I'm going to make my excuses and leave. See if you can get a heart-to-heart with her and find out about that contract. You've been around law offices long enough to be able to spot the joker if you can get a look at it.'

'If she's getting money for putting on weight,' Della Street said wistfully, 'she's living an ideal existence.'

'Until someone jerks the rug out from under her,' Mason said, 'and leaves her with all those curves.'

Della Street smiled. 'I know how easy and rapid it is to put it on and how very slow and painful the process is of taking it off – but what in the world could anybody want with her— Well, you know, I mean *why* would anyone make a contract of that sort?'

Mason said, 'Since she's a friend of your Aunt Mae, it might be a good plan to find out.'

CHAPTER 3

It was nine o'clock the next morning when Mason's phone rang.

'Are you decent?' Della Street asked.

'Fully clothed and in my right mind,' Mason said. 'Where are you?'

'I'm down in the lobby.'

'What gives?'

'The contract.'

'What contract? Oh, you mean with Dianne Alder?'

'Yes.'

'You know what it's all about?'

'I've done better than that. I have her copy with me.'

'Good,' Mason said. 'Come on up. I'll meet you at the elevator.'

Mason met Della and asked, 'Have you had breakfast?'

'No. You?'

Mason shook his head.

'I'm famished,' she said.

'Come on in,' Mason told her, 'and we'll have some sent up to the suite and eat it out on the balcony overlooking the ocean.'

The lawyer called room service and placed an order for a ham steak, two orders of fried eggs, a big pot of coffee, and toast.

Della Street, walking over to the full-length mirror, surveyed herself critically. 'I'm afraid,' she said, 'I'm being inspired by the example of Dianne Alder and am about to go overboard.'

'That breakfast won't be fattening,' Mason said.

'Hush,' she told him. 'I've been at the point where I've even been counting the calories in a glass of drinking water. And now, inspired by the example of Dianne getting paid for putting on weight, I feel that you should supplement that order with sweet rolls and hash-brown potatoes.'

'Shall I?' Mason asked, reaching for the phone.

'Heavens, no!' she exclaimed. 'Here, read this contract and prepare to lose a secretary. Why didn't someone tell me about this sooner?'

'Inspired?' Mason asked.

'To quote a famous phrase,' Della Street said, 'it's nice work if you can get it. I'm thinking of getting it. Eat all you want and get paid for it. Have a guaranteed income. Be free from worries so you can put on weight in the right places.'

'What,' Mason asked, 'are the right places?'

'The places that meet the masculine eye,' she said.

Mason settled in his chair, glanced through the contract, frowned, started reading it more carefully.

By the time the room service waiter arrived with the table and the breakfast order, Mason had completed a study of the contract.

Della Street waited until after the table had been set on the balcony, the waiter had left the room, and Mason had taken the first sip of his coffee.

'Well?' she asked.

Mason said, 'That's the damnedest contract I've ever read.'

'I thought you'd be interested in it.'

'The strange thing,' Mason said, 'is that on its face the contract seems so completely reasonable; in fact, so utterly benevolent. The party of the first part agrees that Dianne may fear she will have trouble getting secretarial employment if she puts on weight, and recognizes the fact that as of the time the contract is signed she is gainfully employed as a secretary in a law office at a salary of five thousand, two hundred dollars a year.

'Since the party of the first part desires that she shall give up that employment and devote herself exclusively to her work as a model, it is guaranteed that she will receive an income of one hundred dollars a week, payable each Saturday morning.

'On the other hand, Dianne, as party of the second part, agrees to put on twelve pounds within a period of ten weeks, to resign her position immediately on the signing of the contract, and loaf on the beach, getting as much of a sun tan as possible.

20

'It is agreed that she will pose in bikini bathing suits as the party of the first part may desire, but she shall not be required to pose in the nude. And if she wishes, at the time of posing in a bikini bathing suit, she may have a woman companion present as her chaperon.

'Now,' Mason went on, 'comes the peculiar part of the contract. It is stated that the parties contemplate that Dianne's total income may greatly exceed the sum of fifty-two hundred dollars a year; that the fifty-two hundred dollars is a minimum guarantee made by the party of the first part; and Dianne is entitled to have that and to keep that income without dividing it. If, however, her income exceeds that amount, she is to share it fifty-fifty with the party of the first part. And, since the party of the first part is taking a calculated risk, it is agreed that Dianne's gross income shall be computed for the purposes of the division as any money she may receive from any source whatever during the life of the contract.

'The contract is to exist for two years, and the party of the first part has the right of renewing it for an additional two years. And, at the expiration of that time, a further right of renewal for another two years.

'During all of the time the contract is in effect any and all monies received from any source whatever by the party of the second part other than the hundred-a-week guarantee are deemed to be gross income which shall be divided equally, whether such income comes from modelling, lecturing on health, posing, television, movies, or from any other source whatever, including prizes in beauty contests, gifts from admirers, or otherwise; inheritances, bequests, devices, or otherwise; and it is recited that the party of the first part having guaranteed her income for the life of the contract, and having made plans to put her in the public eye, and to give her opportunities to greatly increase her income, is entitled to one half of her gross income regardless of the source, and/or whether it is directly or indirectly the result of his efforts on her behalf or of the publicity resulting from his efforts under the contract.'

Mason picked up his knife and fork, divided the ham steak in half, put a piece on Della Street's plate, one on his own, and gave his attention to the ham and eggs.

'Well?' Della Street asked.

'Dianne is a nice girl,' Mason said.

'She has a striking figure,' Della Street said.

Mason nodded.

'She might be described as whistle bait,' Della Street went on.

'Well?' Mason asked.

'Do you suppose the party of the first part is completely unaware of these things?'

Mason said, 'In the course of my legal career I've seen quite a few approaches. I've never seen one quite like this, if that's what the party of the first part has in mind.'

'In the course of my secretarial career,' Della Street said demurely, 'I've seen them *all*, but this is a new one.'

'According to the letter of that contract,' Mason said, 'if Dianne Alder should meet a millionaire, receive a gift of a hundred thousand dollars, and should then marry, or if her husband should die and leave her the million dollars, the party of the first part would be entitled to fifty per cent.'

'Marrying a million dollars is not one of the normal occupational hazards of a legal secretary in a relatively small beach town,' Della Street said.

Suddenly Mason snapped his fingers.

'You've got it?' Della Street asked.

'I have *an* explanation,' Mason said. 'I don't know whether it's *the* explanation but it's quite an explanation.'

'What?' Della Street asked. 'This thing has me completely baffled.'

Mason said, 'Let us suppose that the party of the first part, this Harrison T. Boring, whoever he may be, is acquainted with some very wealthy and rather eccentric person – some person who is quite impressionable as far as a certain type of voluptuous blonde beauty is concerned.

'Let us further suppose Boring has been scouting around, looking for just the girl he wants. He's been spending the summer on the beaches, looking them over in bathing suits. He's picked Dianne as being nearest to type, but she is perhaps slightly lacking in curves.'

'Wait a minute,' Della Street interjected. 'If Dianne's lacking in curves, I'm a reincarnated beanpole.'

'I know, I know,' Mason said, brushing her levity aside. 'But this individual has particular and rather peculiar tastes. He's very wealthy and he likes young women with lots of corn-fed beauty, not fat but, as Dianne expressed it, "firm fleshed".'

'Probably some old goat,' Della Street said, her eyes narrowing.

'Sure, why not?' Mason said. 'Perhaps some rich old codger who is trying to turn back the hands of the clock. Perhaps he had a love affair with a blonde who was exceptionally voluptuous and yet at the same time had the frank, blue-eyed gaze that characterizes Dianne.

'So Boring makes a contract with Dianne. He gets her to put on weight. He gets her to follow his instructions to the letter. At the proper time he introduces her to this pigeon he has all picked out, and from there on Boring takes charge.

'Any one of several things can happen. Either the pigeon becomes involved with Dianne, in which event Boring acts as the blackmailing master-mind who manipulates the shakedown, or the man lavishes Dianne with gifts, or perhaps, if Boring manipulates it right, the parties commit matrimony.'

'And then,' Della Street asked, 'Boring would be getting fifty per cent of Dianne's housekeeping allowance? After all, marriage can be rather disillusioning under certain circumstances.'

'Then,' Mason said, 'comes the proviso that any money she receives within the time limit of the contract, whether by inheritance, descent, bequest, or devise, is considered part of her gross income. Boring arranges that the wealthy husband leads a short but happy life, and Dianne comes into her inheritance with Boring standing around with a carving knife ready to slice off his share.'

Della Street thought that over for a moment. 'Well, what do you know,' she said.

'And that,' Mason said, 'explains the peculiar optional extension provisions of the contract. It can run for two years, four years, or six years at the option of the party of the first part. Quite evidently he *hopes* that the matter will be all concluded with the two-year period, but in the event it isn't and the husband should be more resistant than he anticipates, he can renew the contract for another two years, and if the husband still manages to survive the perils of existence for that four-year period, he can still renew for another two years.'

'And where,' Della Street asked, 'would that leave Dianne Alder? Do you suppose he would plan to have her convicted of the murder?'

'No, no, not that,' Mason said. 'He couldn't afford to.'

'Why not?'

'Because,' Mason pointed out, 'a murderer can't inherit from his victim. Therefore Boring has to manipulate things in such a way that the wealthy husband dies what seems to be a natural death. Or, if murdered, that some other person has to be the murderer. Dianne, as the bereaved widow, steps into an inheritance of a few million dollars, and Boring, as the person who brought Dianne into the public eye and thereby arranged for the meeting with her future husband, produces his contract and wants a fifty-fifty split.'

'With that much involved, wouldn't the contract be contested on the grounds of public policy, undue influence, and a lot of other things?'

'Sure it would,' Mason said, 'but with that much involved and with a contract of this sort in the background, Dianne would make a settlement. If she became a wealthy widow with social possibilities ahead of her, she would hardly want to have this chapter of her career brought into the open; the diet, the putting on weight, the deliberate entrapment of her husband, and all the rest of it.'

'In other words,' Della Street said, 'Harrison T. Boring walked down the beaches looking for a precise type of feminine beauty. When his eyes lit on Dianne, he recognized her as a potential bonanza.'

'Bear in mind,' Mason said thoughtfully, 'that there are certain other things. Dianne has the build of a striptease dancer but essentially has the background of a darn nice girl. Those are the things on which Harrison T. Boring wants to capitalize, and I may point out that the combination is not very easy to come by.

'Usually a girl with Dianne's physical attributes has de-

24

veloped an attitude of sophistication, a certain degree of worldly wisdom, and the unmistakable earmarks of experience, whereas Dianne is essentially shy, self-conscious, easily embarrassed, slightly naïve, and delightfully easy on the eyes.'

'I see that Dianne has impressed you by her good points,' Della Street said.

Mason's eyes were level-lidded with concentration. 'What has Dianne told you about Boring, anything?'

'Very little. She knows very little.

'Dianne was a legal secretary. She was, of course, conscious of her figure. She was also conscious of the fact that if her waist should expand, the rest of her figure would be damaged. So she did a lot of swimming and walking. She would quit work at five o'clock during the summer afternoons, then, taking advantage of daylight saving time, get into her swimming suit, come down on the beach, and walk and swim.'

'Unescorted?' Mason asked.

'She tried to be. She wanted exercise. The average man who wanted to swim with her wasn't particularly keen on that sort of exercise; in fact, very few of them could keep up with her. She walked and ran and swam and, of course, acquired a delightful sun tan.

'Since women of that build like to admire themselves in the nude in front of mirrors, and are painfully conscious of the white streaks which mar the smooth sun tan where convention decrees a minimum of clothing should be worn, Dianne supplemented her weekday swimming parties by lying in the nude in a sun bath she had constructed in the privacy of the back yard.

'About three weeks before this contract was signed she noticed that she was being stared at rather persistently and finally followed by a man whom she describes as being in his thirties, with keen eyes and a dignified, distinguished manner. He looked like an actor.'

'And what happened?'

'Nothing at first. Dianne is accustomed to attracting attention. She's accustomed to having men try to make passes at her and she takes all of that in her stride.

'Then one day Boring approached her and said he had a business proposition he'd like to discuss with her and she told him to get lost. He said that this was purely legitimate; that it had to do with the possibility of her getting gainful employment in Hollywood and was she interested.

'Naturally, Dianne was interested. So Boring gave her this story about a new trend in fashion, about the fact that women were becoming neurotic by paying too much attention to slim figures; that one of the most popular actresses, with women, was Mae West; that if Mae West had only started a new type of dress style it would have gone over like a house on fire; that nature didn't intend women to have thin figures after they had reached maturity as women.

'Dianne said he was very convincing and of course the offer he made was quite attractive.

'All Dianne had to do was to put on weight and put in a lot of time training so that the flesh she put on was firm flesh and not fat. Boring was very insistent about that.'

'All right,' Mason said, 'she signed the contract. Did she get any advice on it? She was working for lawyers and—'

'No, she didn't,' Della Street interjected. 'Boring was particularly insistent that she keep the entire matter completely confidential, that no one should know about it; that under no circumstances was she to mention the reason why she was resigning from her secretarial position.

'Boring explained that he wanted to have this new style of his so highly personalized that women would become aware of Dianne's beauty before they realized they they were being given a new style. Boring said that women were very resistant to new styles until they became a vogue and then they fell all over themselves falling in line.

'Boring has ideas for Dianne to attract a lot of public attention and then he is going to have her put on a series of health lectures. He's going to give her scripts that she is to follow, speeches she is to make, explaining that nature intended a woman to have curves and that men really like women with curves; that the slim, neurotic models are an artificial by-product of the dress designer's art.

'Boring told her that he could set the country on fire with

the right kind of approach to this thing and that all women would throw diets out of the window, start putting on weight, and would only be anxious to have the weight firm flesh instead of bulging fat; that he intended to open up a series of Dianne Alder studios for healthful figures and charming curves.'

Mason said, 'Hang it! The guy could be right at that, Della.'

'It would be a job,' Della said. 'Something you wouldn't want to gamble a hundred dollars a week on.'

'It depends,' Mason said. 'The stakes are big enough . . . All right, now what happened after the contract was signed? Did Boring insist that she become cuddly with him?'

'That is the strange part,' Della Street said. 'Dianne rather felt that that would be a part of the contract and was rather hesitant about it until finally Boring, discovering the reason for her hesitancy, told her that once she signed the contract she would see very little of him; that he was going to be busy in Hollywood, New York, and Paris, laying the foundations for this new type of promotion. So finally Dianne signed the contract.

'She hasn't seen Boring since, but she hears from him on the telephone. Every once in a while he will call her and from the nature of the conversation Dianne knows that he is keeping a close watch on what she is doing.'

'Now, that's interesting,' Mason said.

'Dianne finds it rather disconcerting.'

'How does she receive her hundred dollars, Della?' Mason asked.

'Every Saturday morning there is an envelope in the mail with a cheque. The cheques are signed by the Hollywood Talent Scout Modelling Agency, per Harrison T. Boring, President.'

'Well,' Mason said, 'I don't like to give up a good murder mystery before it's even got off the ground, Della, but there's just a chance this whole idea may be on the up-and-up. Boring's idea sounds pretty far-fetched and fishy when it's written in the cold phraseology of a contract, but the more you think of his explanation, the more plausible it sounds.

'I was hoping that we were on the track of a potential murder before the potential corpse had really walked into the danger zone. I had visions of waiting until Harrison T. Boring had introduced Dianne to his millionaire pigeon and then stepping into the picture in a way that would cause Mr Boring a maximum of embarrassment and perhaps feathering Dianne Alder's nest.'

'As to the latter,' Della Street said, 'we have to remember that every time Dianne's nest gets two feathers, Boring gets one of them.'

'That's what the contract says,' Mason observed, 'but sometimes things don't work out that way ... Well, Della, I guess we'll have to give Mr Harrison T. Boring the benefit of the doubt and you can return Dianne's contract to her. But we'll sort of keep an eye on her.'

'Yes,' Della Street said, 'I thought you would want to do that.'

Mason looked at her sharply but found nothing other than an expression of innocence on her face.

Abruptly the telephone rang. Della Street picked up the instrument.

'Hello,' she said in a low voice. 'This is Mr Mason's suite.'

Dianne Alder's voice came over the phone in a rush of words.

'Oh, Della, I'm glad I caught you!— Your aunt told me where to find you— Della, I have to have that contract back right away. I'm sorry I let you have it and I hope you didn't say anything about it to anybody.'

'Why?' Della asked.

'Because ... well, because I guess I shouldn't have let it out of my possession. There's a proviso in the contract that I'm to do everything I can to avoid premature publicity and— Gosh, Della, I guess I made a booboo even letting you have it or talking about the arrangement. You're the only one I've told anything at all about it. Mr Boring impressed on me that if I started telling even my closest friends, the friends would tell their friends, the newspapers would get hold of it and make a feature story that would result in what he called premature publicity.

'He said that when they got ready to unveil the new models they'd give me a lot of publicity. That was when I was to go on television and they were going to arrange for a movie test, but nothing must be done until they were ready. They said they didn't want irresponsible reporters to skim the cream off their campaign.'

'Do you want me to mail the contract?' Della Street asked.

'If it's all right with you, I'll run up and get it.'

'Whare are you now?'

'I'm at a drugstore only about three blocks from the hotel.'

'Come on up,' Della Street said.

She cradled the phone, turned to Perry Mason, and caught the interest in his eye.

'Dianne?' Mason asked.

'That's right.'

'Wants the contract back?'

'Yes.'

Mason resumed his contemplative study of the ceiling. 'Is she coming up to get the contract, Della?'

'Yes.'

'What caused her sudden concern, Della?'

'She didn't say.'

'When she comes,' Mason said, 'invite her in. I want to talk with her.'

Mason lit a cigarette, watched the smoke curl upward.

At length he said, 'I have become more than a little curious about Harrison T. Boring. He may be smarter than I thought.'

The lawyer lapsed into silence, remained thoughtful until the chimes sounded and Della Street opened the door.

Dianne Alder said, 'I won't come in, Della, thanks. Just hand me the papers and I'll be on my way.'

'Come on in,' Mason invited.

She stood on the threshold as Della Street opened the door wide. 'Oh, thank you, Mr Mason. Thank you so much, but I won't disturb you, I'll just run on.'

'Come in, I'd like to talk with you.'

'I . . .'

Mason indicated a chair.

Reluctantly, apparently not knowing how to avoid the lawyer's invitation without giving offence, Dianne Alder came in and said, 'Actually I'm in a hurry and I ... I didn't want to disturb you. I let Della look over my contract. She was interested and ... well, I wanted to be sure that it was good. You see, I'm depending a lot on that contract.'

'You have dependents?' Mason asked.

'No longer. Mother died over six months ago.'

'Leave you any estate?' Mason asked casually.

'Heavens, no. She left a will leaving everything to me, but there wasn't anything to leave. *I* was supporting *her*. That's why I had to keep on with a steady job. I had thought some of – well, moving to the city, but Mother liked it here and I didn't want to leave her, and it's too far to commute.'

'Father living?'

'No. He died when I was ten years old. Really, Mr Mason, I don't like to intrude on your time, and I – well ... someone is waiting for me.'

'I see,' Mason said, and nodded to Della Street. 'Better give her the contract, Della.'

Dianne took the contract, thanked Della Street, gave Mason a timid hand, said, 'Thank you so much, Mr Mason. It's been such a pleasure meeting you,' and then, turning, walked rapidly out of the door and all but ran down the corridor.

'Well?' Della Street said, closing the door.

Mason shook his head. 'That girl needs someone to look after her.'

'Isn't the contract all right?'

'Is Boring all right?' Mason asked.

'I don't know.'

'He's paying one hundred dollars a week,' Mason said. 'He agrees to pay fifty-two hundred dollars a year. Suppose he doesn't pay it. Then what?'

'Why, he'd be liable for it, wouldn't he?'

'If he has any property,' Mason said. 'It hasn't been determined that he has any property. No one seems to know very much about him.

'Dianne Alder has given up a job. She's putting on weight – that's like rowing out of a bay when the tide is running out.

30

It's mighty easy to go out but when you turn around and try to come back, you have to fight every inch of the way.

'Suppose that some Saturday morning the hundred dollars isn't forthcoming. Suppose she rings the telephone of Harrison T. Boring at the modelling agency and finds the phone has been disconnected?'

'Yes,' Della Street said, 'I can see where that would put Dianne in an embarrassing predicament. But, of course, if she were working at a job, the boss could tell her that he was handing her two weeks' wages and had no further need for her services.'

'He could,' Mason said, 'but if he hired her in the first place and her services were satisfactory, he would have no particular reason to dispense with them.'

'Perhaps Boring would have no reason to dispense with her services,' Della Street said.

'That depends on what he was looking for in the first place,' Mason pointed out. 'If Dianne marries a millionaire, she has to pay over half of what she gets during a six-year period. If Boring quits paying, Dianne may have nothing but an added twelve pounds of weight and a worthless piece of paper.'

Abruptly the lawyer reached a decision. 'Get Paul Drake at the Drake Detective Agency, Della.'

Della Street said, 'Here we go again.'

'We do, for a fact,' Mason said. 'This thing has aroused my curiosity. As an attorney I don't like to stand with my hands in my pockets and watch Dianne being taken for a ride.

'I know I'm getting the cart before the horse, but I'll bet odds that before we get finished Dianne will be asking for our help. When she does, I want to be one jump ahead of Boring instead of one jump behind.'

Della Street said archly, 'Would you be so solicitous of her welfare if she were flat-chested?'

Mason grinned. 'Frankly, Della, I don't know. But I *think* my motivation at the moment is one of extreme curiosity, plus a desire to give Boring a lesson about picking on credulous young women.'

'All right,' she said, 'I'll call Paul. He usually comes into

31

the office around this time on Sundays to check up on the reports made by his various operatives over Friday and Saturday.'

Della Street put through the call. After a few moments she said, 'Hello, Paul . . . The boss wants to talk with you.'

Mason moved over to the telephone. 'Hi, Paul. I have a job for you. A gentleman by the name of Harrison T. Boring. He has a business. It's called the Hollywood Talent Scout Modelling Agency. It's a Hollywood address and that's all I know for sure.'

'What about him?' Drake asked.

'Get a line on him,' Mason said, 'and I'm particularly interested in knowing if he is cultivating some millionaire who has a penchant for young women. If you find any millionaires in the guy's background, I'd like to know about them.

'And it's very important that he has no inkling of the fact he's being investigated.'

'Okay,' Drake said, 'I'll get a line on him.'

'Here's another angle of the same picture,' Mason said. 'Dianne Alder, about twenty-four, with lots of this and that and these and those, blonde, blue-eyed, with lots and lots of figure. Living here at Bolero Beach. Mother died six months ago. Father died when she was ten years old. Worked as a secretary for a law firm. I'm interested in her. She's been living here for some time and it shouldn't be too difficult to get her background. What I am particularly interested in at the moment is finding out whether she's being kept under surveillance.'

'May I ask who your client is?' Drake said. 'I'd like to get the picture in proper perspective.'

'I'm the client,' Mason said. 'Get your men started.'

When Mason had hung up the telephone, Della Street said, 'You think she's under surveillance, Perry?'

'I'm just wondering,' Mason said. 'I'd like to know if someone knew she'd been talking with us and had delivered a warning. She seemed rather disturbed about something. If anyone is playing games, I want to find out about it, and if I'm going to be asked to sit in on the game, I want to draw cards.

32

'Comment?'

Della Street smiled. '*No* comment, but I still wonder what would happen if she'd been flat-chested.'

CHAPTER 4

PERRY MASON had a court hearing set for Monday morning. The hearing ran over until mid-afternoon and it was not until three-thirty that the lawyer reached his office.

Della Street said, 'Paul has a preliminary report on your friend, Harrison T. Boring.'

'Good,' Mason said.

'I'll tell him you're here and he'll give you the low-down.'

Della Street put through the call and a few moments later Paul Drake's code knock sounded on the door of Mason's private office.

Della Street opened the door and let him in.

'Hi, Beautiful,' he said. 'You certainly are a dish with all that beautiful sun tan.'

'You haven't seen it all,' she said demurely.

Mason said, 'She gave *me* an overdose of sun just sitting out on the beach, looking at Dianne Alder. Wait until you see *her*, Paul.'

'I understand from my operatives,' Drake said, 'that Dianne is quite somebody.'

'She certainly cuts a figure,' Della Street said.

'She's a nice kid, Paul,' Mason said, 'and I'm afraid that she's being victimized. What have you found out?'

'Well, of course, Dianne is an open book,' Drake said. 'My operatives quietly nosed around down there at Bolero Beach. She worked for a firm of attorneys, Corning, Chester, and Corning. She hadn't been there too long. She hasn't had too much legal experience but she's an expert typist and shorthand operator. The point is, everyone likes her. The members of the partnership liked her, the clients liked her, and the other two stenographers liked her.

'Then something came along and she quit, but she didn't tell them why she was quitting. She quit almost overnight, simply giving them two weeks' notice.

'She'd been supporting her mother, who had been helpless for some eighteen months prior to her death. It had taken every cent the girl could earn and scrape together to pay the expenses of nursing. She'd work in the office daytimes and then come home and take over the job of being night nurse. It was quite a physical strain and quite a financial drain.'

'No one knew why she had quit?' Mason asked.

'No. She was rather mysterious about the whole thing, simply said she was going to take life a little easier, that she had been working very hard and had been under quite a strain. People who knew what she had been through sympathized with her and were glad to see her relaxing a bit.

'One of the girls in the office thought that Dianne was going to get married but didn't want anyone to know about it. She got that impression simply because of the manner in which Dianne parried questions about what she was going to do and whether she had another job lined up.

'Dianne's father was drowned when she was about ten years old. He and another fellow went off on a trip to Catalina and, like all of these inexperienced guys who start off with outboard motors and open boats, they simply didn't realize the problems they were going to encounter. They ran into head winds apparently; ran out of gas, drifted around for a while, and finally capsized. The Coast Guard found the overturned boat.'

'Bodies?' Mason asked.

'The body of the other man was found, but George Alder's body was never found. That caused complications. At the time there was quite a bit of property, but his affairs were more or less involved, and there was a delay due to the fact that the body wasn't found. However, after a while the court accepted circumstantial evidence that the man had died, and the property, which was community property, went to the wife. She tried to straighten it out so she could salvage something but there were too many complications. And I guess by the time

34

she got through meeting obligations and working out equities, the estate didn't amount to much.

'The mother worked as a secretary for a while and got Dianne through school and then through business college. For a while they both worked and got along pretty well financially. Then the mother had to quit work and finally became ill and was a heavy drag on Dianne during the last years of her life.

'Now then, we start on Harrison T. Boring and there's a different story. Just as it was easy to find out about Dianne, it's hard to find out anything about Boring. The guy has a small account in a Hollywood bank. You can't find out much about it, of course, from the bank, but I did find out that he had references from Riverside, California. I started investigating around Riverside and picked up Boring's back trail there. Boring was in business but no one knew what business. He didn't have an office. He had an apartment and a telephone. He had an account at one of the banks, but the bank either didn't know anything about what he did for a living or wouldn't tell.

'However, we finally ran the guy to earth but we haven't been on the job long enough yet to tell you very much about him. Right at the moment he's somewhere in Hollywood. The place where he has desk space can evidently reach him on the phone whenever it's necessary.

'There's a phone listing under the name of the Hollywood Talent Scout Modelling Agency. It's the same number that's shared by all the clients, and the place where desk space is rented and where mail is answered.

'You wanted to find out about any millionaires in his background. There may be one. Boring has had some business dealings with a George D. Winlock. It's just business, but I don't know the nature of the business.

'Winlock is one of the big shots in Riverside, but he's very shy and retiring, very hard to see; handles most of his business through secretaries and attorneys; has a few close friends and spends quite a bit of his time aboard his yacht which he keeps at Santa Barbara.'

'Did you make any attempt to run down Winlock?'

'Not yet. I don't know very much about him. He drifted

35

into Riverside, went to work as a real estate salesman, worked hard, and was fairly successful. Then he took an option on some property out at Palm Springs, peddled the property, made a neat profit on the deal, picked up more property, and within a few years was buying and selling property right and left. The guy apparently has an uncanny ability to know places that are going up in value.

'Of course, today the desert is booming. Air conditioning has made it possible to live comfortably the year around, and the pure air and dry climate have been responsible for attracting lots of people with a corresponding increase in real estate prices.

'Winlock got right in on the ground floor of the desert boom, and as fast as he could make a dollar he spread it out over just as much desert property as he could tie up. At one time he was spread out pretty thin and was pretty much in debt. Now he's cashing in. He's paid off his obligations and has become quite wealthy.'

'Married?' Mason asked.

'Married to a woman who has been married before and who has a grown son, Marvin Harvey Palmer.

'That's just about all I can tell you on short notice.'

'When did Winlock come to Riverside?' Mason asked.

'I didn't get the date. It was around fifteen years ago.'

Mason drummed with his fingers on the edge of the desk, looked up, and said, 'See what you can find out about Winlock, Paul.'

Drake said, 'What do you want me to do, Perry? Shall I put a man on Winlock?'

'Not at the moment,' Mason said. 'Boring yes, but Winlock, no.'

'I already have a man working on Boring,' Drake said. 'He's in Hollywood at the moment and I've got a man ready to tail him as soon as contact can be made. I can put a round-the-clock tail on him if that's what you want.'

'Probably the one man is sufficient at the moment,' Mason said. 'The point is that he mustn't get suspicious. I don't want him to feel anyone is taking an interest in him.

'What about the Hollywood Talent Scout Modelling

Agency, Paul? Did you get anything on it?'

'It's just a letterhead business,' Drake said. 'The address is at one of those answering-service places where they have a telephone, a secretary, and a business address that serves a dozen or so companies. The whole thing is handled by one woman who rents an office and then sub-rents desk space and gives a telephone-answering, mail-forwarding service.'

'Okay, Paul,' Mason said. 'Stay with it until you find out what it's all about. Remember that technically I don't have any client. I'm doing this on my own so don't get your neck stuck out.'

'Will do,' Drake said and went out in a rush, slamming the door behind him.

Drake had been out of the office less than ten minutes when the phone rang and Della Street relayed the message from the receptionist. 'Dianne Alder is in the office,' she reported.

Mason's frown suddenly lightened into a smile. 'Well, how about that?' he said. 'She's taken the bait and now someone has jerked the line and she's feeling the hook. Go bring her in, Della.'

Della Street nodded, hurried through the door to the reception room, and was back in a few moments with an apologetic Dianne Alder.

'Mr Mason,' she said, 'I know I shouldn't intrude on you without an appointment and I feel just terrible about what happened yesterday; but ... well, the bottom has dropped out of everything and I just *had* to find out what to do.'

'What's happened?' Mason asked.

'A letter,' she said, 'sent registered mail, with a return receipt demanded.'

'You signed the receipt?'

She nodded.

'And the letter is from Boring?' Mason asked.

Again she nodded.

'Telling you that your contract was at an end?'

She said, 'Not exactly. You'd better read it.'

She took a letter from an envelope, unfolded the paper, and handed it to Mason.

Mason read the letter aloud for the benefit of Della Street.

'My dear Miss Alder: I know that as a very attractive young woman you realize the instability of styles and the vagaries of the style designers.

'A few weeks ago when we approached you with the idea of creating a new trend, we felt that there were very great possibilities in the new idea; and, what is more to the point, we had a wealthy backer who agreed with us.

'Now, unfortunately, there has been a change in certain trends which has caused our backer to become decidedly cool to the whole idea and we ourselves now recognize the first indications of a potentially adverse trend.

'Under the circumstances, realizing that you are making great sacrifices in order to put on weight which may be difficult to take off, knowing that you have given up a good job, and feeling that you can very readily either return to that position or secure one equally advantageous, we are reluctantly compelled to notify you that we are unable to go ahead with further payments under the contract.

'If you wish to keep yourself available, and there should be a change in the trend, we will keep you in mind as our first choice, but we feel it would be unfair to you to fail to notify you of what is happening and the fact that we will be unable to continue the weekly payments in the nature of a guarantee.

'Sincerely yours, Hollywood Talent Scout Modelling Agency, per Harrison T. Boring, President.'

Mason studied the letter thoughtfully for a moment, then said, 'May I see the envelope, please, Dianne?'

She handed him the envelope and Mason studied the postmark.

'You received your money Saturday morning?' he asked.

She nodded.

'And this letter was postmarked Saturday morning. Would you mind telling me why you were so anxious to get your contract back yesterday, Dianne?'

'Because I realized that I was not supposed to give out any information about what I was doing and—'

'And someone telephoned you or reminded you of that clause in your contract?'

'No, it was just something that I remembered Mr Boring had said.'

'What?'

'Well, you know I had been working as secretary for a firm of attorneys and he told me that he not only didn't want any publicity in connexion with the contract, and that I wasn't to talk to anyone about it, but he mentioned particularly that he didn't want me to have any attorney friend looking it over, and if I took it to an attorney it would be a very serious breach of confidence.'

'I see,' Mason said.

'So after I let Della take the contract I suddenly realized that if she should show it to you, I would have been violating his instructions and the provisions of the contract. Tell me, Mr Mason, do you suppose there's any chance that he knew what I was doing? That is, that I'd seen you Saturday and that I'd let Della Street look at the contract and—'

Mason interrupted by shaking his head. 'This letter is postmarked eleven-thirty Saturday morning,' he said.

'Oh, yes, that's right. I . . . I guess I felt a little guilty about letting the contract out of my possession.'

'Was there a letter with the cheque you received Saturday morning?'

'No. Just the cheque. They never write letters, just send me the cheque.'

'Did you notice the postmark?'

'No, I didn't.'

'Save the envelope?'

'No.'

'It must have been mailed Friday night,' Mason said, 'if you received it Saturday morning. Now, that means that between Friday night and Saturday noon, something happened to cause Mr Boring to change his mind.'

'He probably learned of some trend in styles which—'

'Nonsense!' Mason interrupted. 'He wasn't thinking about any trend in styles. That contract, Dianne, is a trap.'

'What kind of a trap?'

'I don't know,' Mason said, 'but you will notice the way it's drawn. Boring pays you a hundred dollars a week and gets one half of your gross income from all sources for a period of up to six years if he wants to hold the contract in force that long.'

Dianne said somewhat tearfully, 'Of course I didn't regard this as an option. I thought it was an absolute contract. I thought I was entitled to a hundred dollars a week for two years, at least.'

'That's what the contract says,' Mason said.

'Well then, what right does he have to terminate it in this way?'

'He has no right,' Mason said.

'I'm so glad to hear you say so! That was the way I read the contract, but this letter sounds so – so final.'

'It sounds very final,' Mason said. 'Very final, very business-like, and was intended to cause you to panic.'

'But what should I do, Mr Mason?'

'Give me a dollar,' Mason said.

'A dollar?'

'Yes. By way of retainer, and leave your copy of the contract with me, if you brought it.'

Dianne hesitated a moment, then laughed, opened her purse and handed him a dollar and the folded contract.

'I can pay you – I can pay you for your advice, Mr Mason.'

Mason shook his head. 'I'll take the dollar, which makes you my client,' he said. 'I'll collect the rest of it from Boring or there won't be any charge.'

Mason turned to Della Street. 'Let's see what we can find listed under the Hollywood Talent Scout Modelling Agency, Della.'

A few moments later Della Street said, 'Here they are. Hollywood three, one, five hundred.'

'Give them a ring,' Mason said.

Della Street put through the connexion to an outside line, her nimble fingers whirled the dial of the telephone, and a moment later she nodded to Mason.

Mason picked up his telephone and heard a feminine voice say, 'Hollywood three, one, five hundred.'

'Mr Boring, please,' Mason said.

'Who did you wish to speak with?'

'Mr Boring.'

'Boring?' she said. 'Boring? ... What number were you calling?'

'Hollywood three, one, five hundred.'

'What? ... Oh, yes, Mr Boring, yes, yes. The Hollywood Talent Scout Modelling Agency. Just a moment, please. I think Mr Boring is out of the office at the moment. Would you care to leave a message?'

'This is Perry Mason,' the lawyer said. 'I want him to call me on a matter of considerable importance. I'm an attorney at law and I wish to get in touch with him as soon as possible.'

'I'll try and see that he gets the message just as soon as possible,' the feminine voice said.

'Thank you,' Mason said, and hung up.

He sat for a few moments looking speculatively at Dianne.

'Do you think there's any chance of getting something for me, Mr Mason?'

'I don't know,' Mason said. 'A great deal depends on the set-up of the Hollywood Talent Scout Modelling Agency. A great deal depends on whether I can find something on which to predicate a charge of fraud; or perhaps of obtaining money under false pretences.'

'False pretences?' she asked.

Mason said, 'I don't think Boring ever had the faintest idea of promoting you as a model legitimately. Whatever he had in mind for you was along entirely different lines. He didn't intend to use you to start any new styles, and my best guess is that all of this talk about finding a firm-fleshed young woman who could put on twelve pounds and still keep her curves in the right places was simply so much double-talk.

'I think the real object of the contract was to tie you up so that you would be forced to give Boring a fifty per cent share of your gross income.'

'But I don't have any gross income other than the hundred dollars a week – unless, of course, I could make some because of modelling contracts and television and things of that sort.'

'Exactly,' Mason said. 'There were outside sources of in-

41

come which Boring felt would materialize. Now then, something happened between Friday night and Saturday noon to make him feel those sources of income were not going to materialize. The question is, what was it?'

'But he must have had *something* in mind, Mr Mason. There must have been some tentative television contract or some modelling assignment or something of that sort.'

'That's right,' Mason said. 'There was something that he had found out about; something he wanted to share in; something he was willing to put up money on so he could hold you in line. And then the idea didn't pan out.'

'Well?' she asked.

Mason said, 'There are two things we can do. The obvious, of course, is to get some money out of Boring by way of a settlement. The next thing is to try and find out what it was he had in mind and promote it ourselves.

'Now, I want you to listen very carefully, Dianne. When a person is a party to a contract and the other party breaks that contract, the innocent person has a choice of several remedies.

'He can either repudiate the contract or rescind it under certain circumstances, or he can continue to treat the contract as in force and ask that the other party be bound by the obligations, or he can accept the fact the other party has broken the contract and sue him for damages resulting from the breach.

'All that is in case the element of fraud does *not* enter into the contract. If fraud has been used, there are additional remedies.

'Now, I want you to be very careful to remember that as far as you are concerned the contract is at an end. There are no further obligations on your part under the contract. But we intend to hold Boring for damages because of the breach of the contract. If anyone asks you anything about the contract, you refer them to me. You simply refuse to discuss it. If anyone asks you how you are coming with your diet, or your weight-gaining programme, you tell them that the person with whom you had the contract broke it and the matter is in the hands of your attorney. Can you remember that?'

She nodded.

'Where are you going now? Do you want to stay in town or go back to Bolero Beach.'

'I had intended to go back to Bolero Beach.'

'You have your car?'

'Yes.'

'Go on back to Bolero Beach,' Mason said. 'See that Della has your address and phone number and keep in touch with your telephone. I may want to reach you right away in connexion with a matter of some importance.

'Now, how do you feel about a settlement?'

'In what way?'

'What would you settle for?'

'Anything I could get.'

'That's all I wanted to know,' Mason said. 'You quit worrying about it, Dianne, and incidentally start cutting down on the sweets and developing a more sensible diet.'

She smiled at him and said, 'My clothes are so tight I ... I was just about to get an entirely new wardrobe.'

'I think it'll be cheaper in the long run,' Mason said, 'to start taking off weight.'

'Yes,' she said somewhat reluctantly, 'I suppose so. It's going to be a long uphill struggle.'

CHAPTER 5

It was shortly before five o'clock when Gertie rang Della Street's telephone and Della Street, taking the message, turned to Mason.

'Harrison T. Boring is in the outer office in person.'

'What do you know!' Mason said.

'Do I show him in?'

'No,' Mason said, 'treat him like any other client. Go out, ask him if he has an appointment, get his name, address, telephone number, and the nature of his business, and then show

43

him in. In the meantime slip Gertie a note and have her call Paul Drake, tell him Boring is here and I want him shadowed from the moment he leaves.'

'Suppose he won't give me his telephone number and tell me the nature of his business?'

'Throw him out,' Mason said, 'only be sure there's enough time for Paul to get a tail on him. He's either going to come in the way I want him to or he isn't going to come in at all. My best guess is the guy's scared.'

Della Street left and was gone nearly five minutes. When she returned she said, 'I think he's scared. He gave me his name, telephone number, address, and told me that you had said you wanted to have him call you upon a matter of importance, that rather than discuss it over the telephone he had decided to call in person since he had another appointment in the vicinity.'

'All right,' Mason said. 'Now we'll let him come in.'

Della Street ushered Harrison Boring into the office.

Boring was rather distinguished looking, with broad shoulders, sideburns, keen grey eyes, and a certain air of dignity. He was somewhere in his late thirties, slim-waisted and spare-fleshed, despite his broad shoulders. He had a close-clipped moustache which firmed his mouth.

'Good afternoon, Mr Mason,' he said. 'I came to see you. You asked me to get in touch with you, and since I was here in the neighbourhood on another matter I decided to come in.'

'Sit down,' Mason invited.

Boring accepted the seat, smiled, settled back, crossed his legs.

'Dianne Alder,' Mason said.

There wasn't the faintest flicker of surprise on Boring's face.

'Oh, yes,' he said. 'A very nice young woman. I'm sorry the plans we had for her didn't materialize.'

'You had plans?'

'Oh, yes, very definitely.'

'And made a contract.'

'That's right – I take it you're representing her, Mr Mason?'

44

'I'm representing her.'

'I'm sorry she felt that it was necessary to go to an attorney. That is the last thing I would have wanted.'

'I can imagine,' Mason said.

'I didn't mean it that way,' Boring interposed hastily.

'I did,' Mason said.

'There is nothing to be gained by consulting an attorney,' Boring said, 'and there is, of course, the extra time, trouble, and expense involved.'

'*My* time, *your* trouble, *your* expense,' Mason said.

Boring's smile seemed to reflect genuine amusement. 'I'm afraid, Mr Mason, there are some things about the facts of life in Hollywood you need to understand.'

'Go ahead,' Mason said.

'In Hollywood,' Boring said, 'things are done on front, on flash, on a basis of public relations.

'When a writer or an actor gets to the end of his contract and his option isn't taken up, he immediately starts spending money. He buys a new automobile, purchases a yacht, is seen in all the expensive night spots, and lets it be known that he is at liberty but is thinking of taking a cruise to the South Seas on his yacht before he considers any new contract.

'The guy probably has just enough to make a down payment on the yacht and uses his old automobile as a down payment on the new car. He has a credit card which is good for the checks at the night spots and he's sweating in desperation, but he shows up regularly with good-looking cuties and buys expensive meals. He radiates an atmosphere of prosperity.

'During that time his public relations man is busily engaged in trying to plant stories about him and his agent is letting it be known that while his client has his heart set on a nine to twelve months vacation on his yacht in the South Seas, he *might* be persuaded to postpone the vacation long enough to take on one more job if the pay should be right.

'That's Hollywood, Mr Mason.'

'That's Hollywood,' Mason said. 'So what?'

'Simply, Mr Mason, that I live in Hollywood. I work with Hollywood. I had some elaborate plans. I backed those plans up

45

with what cash I had available and I was able to interest a backer.

'Late Friday night my backer got cold feet on the entire proposition. I hope I can get him re-interested, but I can't do it by seeming to be desperate. I have to put up a good front, I have to let it appear that the loss of his backing was merely a minor matter because I have so many other irons in the fire that I can't be bothered over just one more scheme which could have earned a few millions.'

'And so?' Mason asked.

'And so,' Boring said, 'Dianne would have shared in my prosperity. Now she has to share in my hard luck. If the girl is willing to keep right on going, if she's willing to develop the curves and try to glamorize herself in every way possible, I am hoping that the deal can be reinstated.'

'How soon?'

'Within a matter of weeks – perhaps of days.'

'You mean you hope the backer will change his mind?'

'Yes.'

'Do you have any assurance that he will?'

'I think I can— Well, I'll be perfectly frank, Mr Mason. I think I can guarantee that he'll come around.'

'If you're so certain of it, then keep up your payments to Dianne Alder.'

'I can't do it.'

'Why?'

'I haven't the money.'

Mason said, 'We're not interested in your hard luck. You made a definite contract. For your information, upon a breach of that contract my client could elect to take any one of certain remedies.

'She has elected to consider your repudiation of the contract as a breach of the contractual relationship and a termination of all future liability on her part under the contract. She will hold you for whatever damages she has sustained.'

'Well, I sympathize with her,' Boring said. 'If I were in a position to do so, I'd write her a cheque for her damages right now, Mr Mason. I don't try to disclaim my responsibility in the least. I am simply pointing out to you that I am a pro-

46

moter, I am an idea man. I had this idea and I had it sold. Something happened to unsell my backer. I think I can get him sold again. If I can't, I can get another backer. But every dollar that I have goes into keeping up the type of background that goes with the line of work I'm in. My entire stock-in-trade is kept in my showcases. I don't have any shelves. I don't have any reserve supplies.'

'And you're trying to tell me you don't have any money?' Mason asked.

'Exactly.'

Mason regarded the man thoughtfully. 'You're a salesman.'

'That's right.'

'A promoter.'

'That's right.'

'You sell ideas on the strength of your personality.'

'Right.'

'So,' Mason said, 'instead of talking with me over the telephone, instead of referring me to your attorney, you came here personally to put on your most convincing manner and persuade me that you had no cash and therefore it would be useless for my client to start suit.'

'Correct again, Mr Mason.'

'Do you have an attorney?'

'No.'

'You'd better get one.'

'Why?'

'Because I'm going to make you pay for what you've done to Dianne Alder.'

'You can't get blood out of a turnip, Mr Mason.'

'No,' Mason said, 'but you can get sugar out of a beet – if you know how – and in the process you raise hell with the beet.'

Boring regarded him speculatively.

'Therefore,' Mason said, 'I would suggest that you get an attorney and I'll discuss the situation with him rather than with you.'

'I don't have an attorney, I don't have any money to hire an attorney, and I'm not going to get one. With all due respect to

47

you, Mr Mason, you're not going to get a thin dime out of me; at least, as long as you act this way.'

'Was there some other way you had in mind?' Mason asked.

'Frankly, there was.'

'Let's hear it.'

'My idea is just as good as it ever was. Sooner or later I'm going to get another backer. When I do, Dianne will be sitting on Easy Street. I tell you, Mr Mason, the idea is sound. People are tired of starving their personalities along with their bodies.

'You let some well-nourished, firm-fleshed, clear-eyed model come along that has lots of figure, and we'll start a style change overnight.'

'I'm not an expert on women's styles,' Mason said. 'I try to be an expert on law. I'm protecting my client's legal interests.'

'Go ahead and protect them.'

'All right,' Mason said. 'My client has a claim of damages against you for whatever that may be worth. We won't argue about that now. My client also has the right to consider your repudiation of the contract as a termination of all future liability on her part.'

'I am not a lawyer, Mr Mason, but that would seem to be fair.'

'Therefore,' Mason said, 'regardless of what else may be done, you have no further claims on Dianne Alder, or on her earnings.'

'I'd like to see the situation left in *status quo*,' Boring said.

'*Status quo* calls for the payment of a hundred dollars a week.'

'I can't do it.'

'Then there isn't any *status quo*.'

Boring held out his hand to Mason with a gesture of complete friendship. 'Thank you, Mr Mason, for giving me your time. I'm glad we had this talk. Dianne is a nice girl. You do whatever you can to protect her interests, but I just wanted to let you know that trying to collect from me would simply be throwing good money after bad.'

Boring kept talking while he was shaking hands. 'If I ever

48

get any money of my own, Mason, you won't need to sue me for it because I'd back this idea of mine with every cent I had. It's a red-hot idea and I know it's going to pay off. I realize that the situation is a little discouraging at the moment as far as Dianne is concerned, but I know that sooner or later my idea is going across. I feel in my bones that within a few short months Dianne will be the toast of the town.'

'Let's be very careful,' Mason said, moving Boring towards the exit door, 'that the toast doesn't get burnt.'

'I can assure you, Mr Mason, with every ounce of sincerity I possess, that I have her best interests at heart.'

'That's fine,' Mason said, 'and you can be assured that I have them at heart.'

Mason held the exit door open for Boring, who smiled affably, then turned and walked down the corridor.

Mason turned to Della Street as the door closed. 'You got Paul Drake?' he asked.

'That's right. He'll be under surveillance from the time he leaves the building. One of Drake's operatives will probably be in the elevator with him as he goes down.'

Mason grinned.

'Quite a promoter,' Della Street said.

Mason nodded. 'That damned contract,' he said.

'What about it?'

'I wish I knew what Boring was after. I wish I knew the reason he drew up that contract in the first place.'

'You don't believe his story about a new type of model and—'

Mason interrupted to say, 'Della, I don't believe one single damn thing about that guy. As far as I'm concerned, even his moustache could be false— Get me that contract, will you, Della? I want to study it once more.'

Della Street brought him the file jacket. Mason took out the contract and read it carefully.

'Any clues?' Della Street asked.

Mason shook his head. 'I can't figure it out. It's . . .'

Suddenly he stopped talking.

'Yes?' Della Street prompted.

'Well, I'll be damned!' Mason said.

'What?' Della Street asked.

'The red herring is what fooled me,' Mason said.

'And what's the red herring?'

'The avoirdupois, the diet, the twelve pounds in ten weeks, the curves.'

'That wasn't the real object of the contract?' Della Street asked.

'Hell, no,' Mason said. 'That was the window dressing. That was the red herring.'

'All right, go ahead,' she said. 'I'm still in the dark.'

'Take that out of the contract,' Mason said, 'and what do you have left? We've seen these contracts before, Della.'

'I don't get it.'

'The missing-heir racket,' Mason said.

Della Street's eyes widened.

Mason said, 'Somebody dies and leaves a substantial estate, but no relatives. No one takes any great interest in the estate at the moment except the public administrator.

'Then these sharpshooters swoop down on the situation. They start feverishly running down all the information they can get on the descendant. They find that some relatives are living in distant parts, relatives who have entirely lost track of the family connexion.

'So these sharpshooters contact the individual potential heirs and say, "Look here. If we can uncover some property for you which you didn't know anything at all about, will you give us half of it? We'll pay all the expenses, furnish all the attorneys' fees out of our share. All you have to do is to accept your half, free and clear of all expenses of collection."'

'But who's the relative in this case?' Della Street asked. 'Dianne's family is pretty well accounted for. Her father died, and all of the estate, such as it was, was distributed to her mother, and then her mother died, leaving everything to Dianne.'

'There could be property inherited from the more remote relatives,' Mason pointed out. 'That's where these sharpies make their money.'

'Then why would he quit making the payments to her and forfeit all right to her share of the money?'

'Either because he found out she wasn't entitled to it,' Mason said, 'or because he's found another angle he can play to greater advantage.'

'And if he has?' Della Street asked.

'Then,' Mason said, 'it's up to us to find out what he's doing, block his play, and get the inheritance for Dianne, all without paying him one thin dime.'

'Won't that be quite a job?' Della Street asked.

'It'll be a terrific job,' Mason said. 'We're going to have to get hold of Dianne and start asking her about her family on her father's side and her mother's side, her cousins, aunts, second cousins, uncles, and all the rest of it. Then we've got to start running down each person to find out where they're located, when they died, where they died, what estate was probated, and all the rest of it.

'There is, however, one method of short-cutting the job.'

'What's that?'

'By shadowing Boring, checking back on where he's been, what he's been doing, and, if possible, with whom he's corresponding – and that's a job for Paul so we'll let Paul wrestle with it until he gets a lead.

'Come on, Della, let's close up the office and forget about business for a change. We may as well call it a day.'

Della Street nodded.

Mason opened the exit door, started to go out, suddenly paused, and said, 'Della, there's someone rattling the knob of the door of the reception office – would you mind slipping out and telling him that we're closing up and see if we can make an appointment with this man for tomorrow.'

A few moments later she was back in the office. 'You may want to see this man, Chief,' she said.

'Who is it?'

'His name is Montrose Foster and he wants to talk to you about Harrison T. Boring.'

'Well, well!' Mason said, grinning. 'Under the circumstances, Della, I guess we'll postpone closing the office until we've talked with Mr Montrose Foster, following which we could, if so desired, dine uptown and perhaps invite Paul Drake to go to dinner with us.

'Bring him in.'

Within a few seconds Della Street was back with a wiry, thin-faced individual whose close-set, black, beady eyes were restlessly active. He had high cheekbones, a very prominent pointed nose, quick, nervous mannerisms, and rapid enunciation.

'How do you do, Mr Mason, how do you do?' he said. 'I recognize you from your photographs. I've always wanted to meet you.

'Tops in the field, that's what you are, sir, tops in the field. It's a pleasure to meet the champion.'

'What can I do for you?' Mason asked, sizing the man up with good-natured appraisal.

'Perhaps we can do something for each other, Mr Mason. I'll put it that way.'

'Well, sit down,' Mason said. 'It's after hours and we were just closing up. However, if you'll be brief, we can make a preliminary exploration of the situation.'

'My interest is in Harrison T. Boring,' Foster said, 'and I have an idea that you're interested in him.'

'And if so?' Mason asked.

'I think we could pool our information, Mr Mason. I think I could be of some assistance to you and you might be of some assistance to me.'

'Where do we begin?' Mason asked.

'I happen to know – and never mind how I happen to know it – that you left word for Harrison Boring to get in touch with you. I happen to know that Mr Boring picked up that message and in place of calling you on the telephone as apparently you wished him to do, came here in person. I happen to know that he left here only a short time ago. And, if you'll forgive me, that was the reason I was so persistently trying to attract attention by knocking at the door of your reception room. I felt certain you were still here.'

'I see,' Mason said.

'Now then,' Foster went on, 'if you'll let me have the name of your client, Mr Mason, I think I can perhaps be of help to you.'

'And why do you wish the name of my client?'

'I'm simply checking, Mr Mason, to make certain that I'm on the right track.'

Mason's eyes narrowed slightly. 'I fail to see what good it would do to divulge the name of my client. If, of course, you wish to tell me anything about Boring, I'm ready to listen.'

'Boring,' Foster said, 'is an opportunist, a very shrewd character, very shrewd.'

'Unscrupulous?' Mason asked.

'I didn't *say* that,' Foster said.

'May I ask how you know so much about him?'

'The man worked for me for a period of two years.'

'In what capacity?' Mason asked.

'He was a – well, you might say an investigator.'

'And what is your line of work?' Mason asked.

Foster became elaborately casual. 'I have several activities, Mr Mason. I am a man of somewhat diverse interests.'

'The principal one of which,' Mason said, making a shot in the dark, 'is locating missing heirs. Is that right?'

Foster was visibly shaken. 'Oh,' he said, somewhat crestfallen, 'you know about that, do you?'

'Let's put it this way, I surmised it.'

'And why did you surmise that, may I ask?'

'The fact that you were so interested in the name of my client, Mr Foster.'

Foster said somewhat sheepishly, 'I may have been a little abrupt but, after all, I was trying to help *you*, Mr Mason. That was what I primarily had in mind.'

'And, at the same time, helping yourself to a piece of cake,' Mason said. 'Let's see if I can reconstruct the situation. You're running an agency for the location of lost heirs. Boring was working for you. All of a sudden he resigned his position and started quietly investigating something on his own.

'You felt certain that this was some information he had uncovered in the course of his employment and something on which he was going to capitalize to his own advantage. You have been making every effort to find out what the estate is, and who the missing heir is, and hope you can get the information before Boring signs anyone up on a contract.'

53

Montrose Foster seemed to grow smaller by the second as Mason was talking.

'Well,' he said at length, 'I guess you've either found out all there is to know or else you got Boring in such a position you were able to turn him inside out.'

'What was the matter on which Boring was working when he quit you?' Mason said. 'Perhaps that would be a clue.'

'That's a clue and a very nice one,' Foster said, 'and it's a very nice question, Mr Mason, but I'm afraid we've reached a point where we're going to have to trade. You give me the name of the client and I'll give you the name of the estate on which Boring was working.'

Mason thought things over for a moment, then slowly shook his head.

'It might save you a lot of time,' Foster said pleadingly.

'That's all right,' Mason told him. 'I'll spend the time.'

'It will cost a lot of money.'

'I have the money.'

'You give me the name of your client,' Foster said, 'and if that client hasn't already signed up with Boring, I'll run down the matter for twenty-five per cent. Surely, Mr Mason, you can't expect anything better than that. Our usual fee is fifty per cent and that's in cases which don't involve a great deal of work.'

'Well,' Mason said, 'I'll take your offer under advisement.'

'There isn't time, Mr Mason. This is a matter of considerable urgency.'

Mason said, 'I don't do any horse trading until I've seen the horse I'm trading for.'

'I've put my cards on the table.'

'No, you haven't. You haven't told me anything about yourself except to confess that the information you've been able to uncover has not been anything on which you could capitalize.'

'All right, all right,' Foster said. 'You're too smart for me, Mr Mason. You keep reading my mind, so to speak. I *will* put the cards on the table. If I could find the name of the heir, I'd start running it down from the other end and then I'd find it. As it is, you're quite correct in assuming that I haven't been

54

able to get any satisfaction from checking over the estates which Boring was investigating.'

'And you've talked with Boring?' Mason asked. 'Offered to pool your information? Offered him a larger commission than you customarily granted?'

'Yes. He laughed at me.'

'And then what happened?'

'Then I'm afraid I lost my temper. I told him what I thought of him in no uncertain terms.'

'And what were the no uncertain terms?'

'The man is a liar, a cheat, a sneak, a double-crosser, a back-stabber, and entirely unscrupulous. He puts up a good front but he's nothing more than a con man. He worked for me, let me carry him during all the lean times, then just as soon as he stumbled on to something juicy he manipulated things so he could put the whole deal in his pocket and walk off with it.'

Mason flashed Della Street a quick glance. 'I take it you didn't have him tied up under contract. Therefore, there wasn't any reason why he couldn't quit his employment and go to work on his own, so I can't see why you're so bitter.'

'This wasn't something he did on his own, Mason. Don't you understand? This was something he uncovered while he was working for me. I was paying him a salary and a commission and he stumbled on to this thing and then, instead of being loyal to his employer and his employment, he sent me a letter of resignation and started developing it himself.'

'If you don't know what it was,' Mason asked, 'how do you know it was something he uncovered as a part of his employment?'

'Now look,' Foster said, 'you're pumping me for a lot of information. I know what you're doing, but I have no choice except to ride along in the hope that you will see the advantages of cooperating with me.'

'I'm afraid,' Mason said, 'I don't see those advantages clearly, at least at the present.'

'Well, think them over,' Foster said. 'You let me know the name of your client and I'll start chasing down the thing from that angle. I have facilities for that sort of investigative work. That's my specialty.'

'And then you'll want half of what my client gets?' Mason asked.

'I told you I'll make a deal with you, Mason. I'll take twenty-five per cent and I'll do all the work. You can take twenty-five per cent as your fee and then your client will get the other half. Is that fair?'

'No.'

'What's unfair about it?'

'If I don't do any of the work,' Mason said, 'I shouldn't charge my client twenty-five per cent of the inheritance.'

'Well, you've got to live,' Foster said.

'With myself,' Mason pointed out, smiling.

'Oh, all right, all right. Think it over,' Foster said. 'You're going to be doing business with me sooner or later anyway.'

'How so?'

'Because I'm going to find out what Boring is working on if it takes my last cent. I'm going to see to it that he doesn't profit by his double-crossing.'

'That's a very natural attitude for you to take,' Mason said, 'if you want to spend the effort and money.'

'I've got the time, I've got the money, I'll make the effort,' Foster said. 'Think my proposition over, Mr Mason. Here's one of my cards. I'm located in Riverside. *You* can reach me on the phone at any time, day or night. Call the office during the daytime, and the night number is my residence.'

'Thanks a lot,' Mason said. 'I'll think it over.'

As Della Street held the corridor door open for Montrose Foster, he twisted his head with a quick, terrier-like motion, wreathed his face into a smile, and hurried out into the corridor.

The door slowly closed behind him and Della Street turned to Mason.

'The plot thickens,' she said.

'The plot,' Mason said, frowning thoughtfully, 'develops lumps similar to what my friend, on a camping trip, called Thousand Island gravy.'

'Well?' she asked.

'Let's start taking stock of the situation,' he said. 'Foster was the brains behind a lost heirs organization. He dug out the

56

cases and carried the financial burden. Boring, with his impressive manner and his dignified approach, was the contact man.

'Now then, if any unusual case had been uncovered, if any information had been turned up, one would think Foster would have been the man to do it, not Boring.'

'I see your point,' Della Street said.

'Yet Boring is the one who turns up the case and, despite the fact that Foster had been directing his activities, Foster doesn't have a single lead as to what the case is. So now Foster is desperately trying to find out who the heir is and start back-tracking from that angle.'

'Well,' Della Street said, 'it's a tribute to your thinking that you figured it out this far, largely from studying the contract.'

'*I'm* not handing myself any bouquets,' Mason said. 'I should have figured it out sooner ... Now then, Foster is evidently having Boring shadowed.'

'Otherwise he wouldn't have known he came here?'

Mason nodded.

'And we're having Boring shadowed,' Della Street said.

'Shadows on shadows,' Mason told her. 'Come on, Della, we're going to have dinner on the office expense account and think things over. Then I'll drive you home.'

'Cocktails?' Della Street asked, with a smile.

'The works,' Mason said. 'Somehow I feel like celebrating. I love to get into a situation where everyone is trying to double-cross everyone else.'

'What about Dianne? Do we talk with her and tell her what we have discovered?'

'Not yet,' Mason said. 'We do a little thinking first; in fact, we do a lot of thinking.'

A ROUTINE COURT hearing on Tuesday morning developed into a legal battle which ran over into the afternoon and it was three-thirty that afternoon before Mason checked in at his office.

'Hello, Della,' the lawyer said. 'What's new?'

'Mostly routine,' she said. 'How did the court hearing go?'

Mason grinned. 'Things were looking pretty black and then the attorney on the other side started arguing with the judge over a minor point and the argument progressed to a point where there was a considerable heat on both sides. By the time the hearing was finished the judge decided it our way.'

'And what did you do?' she asked, with exaggerated innocence. 'I suppose you just stood there with your hands in your pockets while the attorney and the judge were arguing.'

'I tried to act the part of a peacemaker,' Mason said. 'I poured oil on the troubled flames.'

Della Street laughed. 'I'll bet you did just that.'

'What's new with our case involving the curvaceous blonde, Della?'

'There seems to be a lot of activity centring in Riverside,' she said. 'Paul Drake reports that Harrison Boring has gone to Riverside. He is now registered in the Restawhile Motel and is in Unit 10.

'Drake's man also reports that Boring is being shadowed by another agency.'

'You mean he's wearing two tails and doesn't know about either one?' Mason asked.

'Apparently not,' Della Street said. 'Of course, under the circumstances Drake's man is being *most* discreet and is relying as much as possible on electronic shadowing devices which send out audible signals to the car following. He thinks the other agency is using contact observation with no electronic shadowing. So far, Boring apparently isn't suspicious. Paul says the man is hurrying around, covering a lot of territory.'

Mason settled back in his swivel chair. 'Hurrying around, eh?' he said musingly.

'Here's the mail,' Della Street said, sliding a stack of letters across Mason's desk.

Mason picked up the top letter, started to read it, put it down, then pushed the pile of mail to one side, sat for more than a minute in thoughtful silence.

'Something?' Della Street asked.

'I'm toying with an idea,' Mason said, 'and hang it, the more I think of it, the more plausible it seems.'

'Want to talk it out or let it incubate?' she asked.

'I think I'd like to talk it out,' Mason said, 'and let's see if it isn't logical. Boring was working on lost heirs, obscure estates. Yet when Foster tried to back-track his activities, he couldn't find anything. Nevertheless, Foster is a pretty thorough-going chap and he has the inside track. In the first place, he knows all the routine methods of investigation and in the second place he knew exactly where Boring had been and what activities he had engaged in. Yet nothing that he has been able to uncover gives any clue to what triggered Boring's break with him.'

Della Street, knowing that Mason was simply thinking out loud, sat thoughtfully attentive, furnishing him with a silent audience.

'So suddenly Harrison T. Boring comes to Dianne Alder,' Mason said, 'and ties her up on a contract, but the contract is so disguised that neither she nor anyone else who might look at the contract would tumble to the fact that it was a lost heir's contract; the sugar-coating disguised the pill to such an extent that the whole thing looked like a piece of candy.'

Della Street merely nodded.

'Now then,' Mason went on, 'Montrose Foster. Regardless of the fact that he's a little terrier, but no one's dummy, he begins to think that perhaps he should start working on the case from the other end and is anxious to find out who Boring has been seeing.'

Again Della Street nodded.

'He is having Boring shadowed. He undoubtedly knows that Boring is seeing Winlock. But Winlock doesn't seem to be the solution to the problem, at least as far as Foster is concerned.

'Now, that's where we're one step ahead of Montrose Foster. We know that whatever lead Harrison Boring may have uncovered, he followed it to Dianne Alder. Dianne Alder is the target in the case, the pot of gold at the end of the rainbow.'

Mason was silent for a few seconds, then he said, 'Yet, having found Dianne Alder and having tied her up, Boring suddenly lets her go.

'Now, why?'

Della Street merely sat looking at him, making no comment.

'The reason is, of course,' Mason said, 'that the advantage Boring intended to get from his contract with Dianne – and that must have been a considerable advantage for him to put out a hundred dollars a week – has been superseded by something much more profitable to Harrison Boring.'

'Such as what?' Della Street asked.

'Blackmail.'

'Blackmail!' she exclaimed.

'That's right,' Mason said. 'He started out on a missing heir's contract and he suddenly shifted to blackmail. That is about the only explanation that would account for his going to all that trouble to sign Dianne up on a missing heir's contract and then suddenly drop her.'

'But why would blackmail tie in with missing heirs?' she asked.

'Because,' Mason said, 'we've been looking at the whole picture backwards. There aren't any missing heirs.'

'But I thought you just said Dianne was a missing heir.'

'We may have started in with that idea,' Mason said, 'but it's a false premise and that's why we aren't getting anywhere, and that's why Montrose Foster isn't getting anywhere. Dianne Alder isn't a missing heir; this is a case of a missing testator.'

'What do you mean?'

'Dianne's father was killed some fourteen years ago, drowned accidentally while boating in the channel, but his body was never found.'

'Then, you mean? . . .'

'I mean,' Mason said, 'that his body wasn't found because he wasn't dead. He was rescued in some way and decided to leave the impression that he was dead. He went out and began life all over and probably amassed something of a fortune.

'He probably was tired of his home life, wanted to disappear the way many men do, but never had the opportunity until that boating accident.'

'So then?' Della Street asked, with sudden excitement.

'So then,' Mason said, 'we start looking for a wealthy man – someone who has no background beyond fourteen years ago, someone who couldn't divorce his wife because he was supposed to be dead, someone who has since remarried, someone who is exceedingly vulnerable, therefore, to blackmail.

'Dianne, as his daughter, would have a claim which could be enforced.'

'But didn't Dianne's mother take all of the estate?' Della Street asked.

'All that she knew about,' Mason said. 'All the estate that Dianne's father left *at the time of his disappearance*. But technically he was still married to Dianne's mother. Technically anything that he acquired after his disappearance and before the death of Dianne's mother was community property.'

'Then,' Della Street said, with sudden excitement, 'the key to the whole thing is George D. Winlock.'

'Exactly,' Mason said. 'Winlock, the wealthy man whom Harrison Boring is cultivating at the moment; Winlock, the real estate speculator who showed up in Riverside about fourteen years ago as a salesman, who started plunging in real estate, became wealthy, and is now one of the town's leading citizens; Winlock, who has a high social position, a wife who really isn't a wife . . . No wonder Boring was willing to let Dianne off the hook! He had landed a bigger fish.'

'I take it,' Della Street said, 'that we go to Riverside.'

Mason grinned. 'Get your things packed, Della. Put in some notebooks and pencils. We go to Riverside.'

'And we see George D. Winlock?'

'We make some very careful investigations,' Mason said,

'and we are very, very careful indeed not to upset any apple carts, not to make any accusations, not to jump to any false conclusions, but very definitely we see George D. Winlock.'

'And when we see him?'

'We see him as Dianne Alder's attorney, and the minute we do that I think you will find that Harrison T. Boring's blackmail has been dried up at the source. And, since Boring has repudiated his contract with Dianne, whatever we can get for her by way of a settlement will be pure velvet to her.

'How long will it take you to get some things packed, Della?'

She smiled. 'Five minutes. I've been through this same thing so often that I'm now keeping an overnight bag in the coat closet.'

CHAPTER 7

SID NYE, Paul Drake's right-hand man, was waiting for Perry Mason when he and Della Street arrived at the colourful Mission Inn Hotel in Riverside.

'Hello, Sid,' Mason said, shaking hands. 'You know Della Street. What's new?'

'Something I want to talk over with you,' Nye said. 'I talked with Paul on the phone and said you were on your way up here and should be here any minute.'

Della Street filled out the registration cards, and Mason, Nye, and Della were shown up to the lawyer's suite. Mason ordered a round of drinks, and Nye, settling himself comfortably in the chair, said, 'The fat seems to be in the fire.'

'Just what happened?' Mason asked.

'I don't know all of the ramifications of the case,' Nye said, 'but it seems that you were having a Harrison T. Boring shadowed.'

'That's right. What happened?'

'Apparently he got wise that he was being tailed, but it wasn't our fault. There was another man following him, and Boring first became suspicious because the other man was using contact shadowing.'

'Go ahead,' Mason said.

'You remember Moose Dillard?' Nye asked.

Mason frowned, then said, 'Oh, yes. I place him now. The big fellow that I represented when he was in a jam over losing his licence.'

'That's right. That was when he lost his temper and flattened a politician who was calling him names. Personally I think the politician had it coming to him, but that's neither here nor there. The guy had political influence and Dillard has a hell of a temper. Anyway, Moose Dillard was tailing Boring. He put an electronic bug on Boring's car so the tailing could be done without giving Boring any cause for alarm, and there's no reason on earth Boring should have known he was being shadowed if it hadn't been for this other man using contact methods.

'Well, Boring spotted the other shadow and started out to ditch him, and did a good job of it. That other shadow was left way back in Hollywood somewhere, but it made Boring shadow conscious.

'Of course, with our electronic tailing devices, Moose Dillard had no trouble. Anyhow, when a guy once gets suspicious, Dillard is such a big guy it's hard to forget him. A tail should be an inconspicuous fellow who can mingle with the crowd, and Dillard has always had a little trouble fading out because of his build, but he's the best automobile tail in the business. He's a genius at handling a car. He wraps those big hands of his around the steering wheel and the car seems to be a part of him.'

Mason nodded. 'What happened?'

'Well, Boring decided to come back to Riverside. I don't know what it was, probably a telephone conversation he had with someone. Anyway, he was in Hollywood, then he threw a suitcase into his car and started out at high speed. He cut figure eights and lost the other shadow. Dillard kept on his tail. After they hit the freeway, Dillard kept pretty well in the background, relying on the electronic device to keep him posted.'

'And what happened?'

'Boring went to Winlock's office, then to the Restawhile Motel here and registered in Unit 10. Dillard waited awhile, then registered and got Unit Number 5, which is across the way from Unit 10 and would give a pretty good view of Boring's place.

'Now, here's the peculiar thing: Dillard checked in and drew the curtains across the window but left just a little crack in the curtain so he could see out, and after a while he saw Boring come out, cross over directly to Dillard's automobile, open the door, and start prowling around.'

'What did Dillard do?'

'He sat tight. He said he was inclined to go out and grab the guy by the collar and give him a good shaking but he remembered the trouble he'd been in before, so he just sat in there and took it.'

'What was Boring looking for?'

'Presumably he was suspicious of Dillard and wanted to find out something about the registration of the automobile.'

'Did he learn anything?'

'That's anybody's guess. The registration is in the name of Paul Drake as an individual and, of course, in order to comply with California law there's a certificate of registration in a cellophane window strapped to the steering wheel.'

'So Dillard sat tight?'

'Dillard sat tight but he's afraid he's been spotted and he wants instructions.'

Mason thought for a minute, then said, 'Tell him to stay right there in the unit and keep his eye on the unit where Boring is staying. I want to know everyone who comes to see Boring and I want to know what time Boring goes out.'

'But suppose Boring does go out. Does Dillard try to shadow him?'

'No,' Mason said. 'It would be too dangerous under the circumstances. He'd be spotted even if he was using an electronic shadowing device. He'll just have to sit tight.'

'The guy hasn't had any dinner,' Nye said. 'He's a big guy and he gets hungry.'

'Well, I don't want to take a chance on letting him go out, at any rate while Boring is there. Do you folks have a good woman operative up here?'

'Not up here but we could probably get one. What do you want?'

'A good-looking woman could go into Dillard's apartment looking as though she were some married woman on a surreptitious date and probably smuggle Dillard in something to eat. It wouldn't be what he wants, but she could get some hamburgers and a Thermos jug of coffee and carry them in. Then if Boring is turning the tables on Dillard and keeping an eye on Dillard's apartment, the fact that this woman goes in there with just the right furtive attitude will probably reassure Boring and, at the same time, give Dillard something to eat.'

'Can do,' Nye said. 'But it will take a couple of hours.'

'Anything else new?' Mason asked.

'That seems to be it at the moment, but probably you'd better call Paul, let him know that you're here and that you and I have been in touch – or would you rather I just reported to Paul?'

'No, I'll call him,' Mason said. 'Get him on the phone, Della.'

Mason turned back to Nye and said, 'Sit back and relax and tell me something about George Winlock, because I'm going to talk with the guy.'

'There isn't much to tell. He's a chap who came here about fourteen years ago and got a job as a real estate salesman. He was a hard worker and a good salesman. He made a couple of big commissions; then he had a chance to tie up some property that he thought was good subdivision property and instead of simply taking a listing on it he took an option – paid every cent he had for a ninety-day option, then got busy and peddled it for a hundred thousand profit. From that time on he started pyramiding. The guy has brains, all right, and he's a shrewd operator. But he keeps pretty much in the background.'

'What about his wife?'

'She's inclined to be just a little snooty; puts on airs, is just a little bit patronizing as far as the local society is concerned, and while they kowtow to her because of her social position, I have a feeling she wouldn't win any popularity contests if there was a secret ballot, but she'd probably be elected Queen of the May if the feminine voters had to stand up and be counted.'

'What about her son?'

'Marvin Harvey Palmer is one of those things,' Nye said. 'We're getting too many of them. He apparently feels that there's never going to be the slightest necessity for him to do any work and he doesn't intend to try. He's an addict for sports cars, a devil with the women, has been picked up a couple of times for drunk driving, but has managed to square the rap somewhere along the line and— Oh, hell, Perry, you know the picture.'

Della Street said, 'Here's Paul Drake on the line, Chief.'

Mason crossed over to the telephone.

Drake said, 'Hello, Perry. I'm going to give you a description of a man and you can tell me if it means anything to you.'

'Go ahead.'

'Five foot eight or nine; weight about a hundred and thirty-five pounds, bony shoulders; high cheekbones; very dark but rather small eyes, and a pointed nose that's quite prominent. He's in his late thirties or early forties, quick-moving, nervous—'

'You are describing Mr Montrose Foster,' Mason interrupted. 'He's the president of Missing Heirs and Lost Estates, Incorporated, and he called on me trying to pump me for information. Harrison Boring worked for him before branching out on his own.'

'He's found Dianne Alder.'

'The hell he has.'

'That's right.'

'How did he find her?'

'I'm darned if I know, Perry. He nosed her out some way. The guy probably is pretty smart. He seems to be a fast worker.

'I think he traced Harrison Boring to Bolero Beach and when he got to inquiring around Bolero Beach he found out that Boring was interested in Dianne Alder.

'Now, it's anybody's guess whether Foster did a little snooping around and found out what Boring's deal with Dianne was, and took it from there; or whether he decided to work fast and go shake Dianne down and see what she'd tell him.

'One thing is certain. Dianne became very much upset as a result of his visit, and shortly after he left, Dianne got her car and drove off in a rush.'

'You're not having her tailed?' Mason asked.

'No. You didn't tell me to. As it happened, the Bolero Beach operative who was nosing around on Boring's back track happened to learn that this character with the pointed nose had been making inquiries about Boring, and so he tried to pick the guy up. He ran into him just as Foster was leaving Dianne's apartment. Then Dianne came out within about ten minutes, jumped in her car, and took off in a hurry.'

'How long ago?'

'An hour or an hour and a half.'

Mason said, 'Your man, Moose Dillard, who was shadowing Boring, seems to have attracted Boring's attention. Boring detected the other tail he was wearing and then spotted Dillard when Dillard registered in the Restawhile Motel. He went over to take a look at Dillard's automobile. The car is registered in your name.'

'So I understand,' Drake said. 'I have a report on it. What are you goind to do about Dillard?'

'I'm talking with Sid Nye now,' Mason said. 'Sid is in my suite here in the hotel. I told him to have Dillard stay put. We'll get some woman operative to look as though she's keeping a motel date with him, and take some sandwiches and a Thermos jug of coffee in to him. He can, of course, get a line on anyone who comes to see Boring there at the motel but his efficiency is pretty much impaired as far as we're concerned.'

'How about putting another shadow on Boring?'

'I don't know,' Mason said. 'I don't think it's going to be necessary. I've decided to cut the Gordian knot by getting in touch with the man about whom this whole thing revolves.'

'Who's that?'

'George D. Winlock.'

'Winlock!' Drake said.

'Right.'

'You've decided he's the one Dianne was picked out for?'

'No. I'm approaching the problem from another angle, Paul. I've come to the conclusion Winlock holds the key to the entire situation.'

'Can you discuss it over the phone?'

'No,' Mason said. 'I'll have to quarterback it from here, Paul.'

'Okay,' Drake said. 'You're on the ground up there and Nye is in charge of the forces up there. You just go ahead and tell Sid what you want done ... Do you want my men on the job down there in Bolero Beach any more?'

'No, call them off,' Mason said. 'I'll tell Sid what to do.'

As Mason hung up the phone, Sid said, 'Well, I'll get busy and get some good-looking gal lined up who can take some dinner in to Dillard. Dillard has a phone in his room and can call out, but we have to play it easy because the line goes through a switchboard there at the motel and there's always the chance the manager may be listening in.'

'Where can I reach you if I should want you in a hurry?' Mason asked.

'The best way is through the office of the Tri-Counties Detective Agency. They're our correspondents up here and we cooperate with them down at our end of the line and they handle things up here.'

'Okay,' Mason said. 'I'll be in touch with you.'

'You're going to see this man Winlock?'

'I'm going to try to.'

'He's a pretty shrewd operator,' Nye said. 'He plays them close to his chest.'

Mason nodded to Della Street. 'See if you can get him on the line, Della.'

'Maybe I'd better wait here until you find out what's cooking,' Nye said.

Della Street consulted the telephone book, put through the call, and nodded to Perry Mason. 'Mr Winlock,' she said, 'this is the secretary of Mr Perry Mason, an attorney of Los Angeles. Mr Mason would like to talk with you. Will you hold the phone just a moment, please?'

Mason took the phone which Della Street extended to him, said, 'Hello, Mr Winlock. Perry Mason talking.'

Winlock's voice was cold and cautious. 'I've heard of you, Mr Mason,' he said. 'And I have seen you. I was in the courthouse very briefly one time when you were trying a case up here in Riverside.'

'I see,' Mason said. 'I would like to have a few minutes of your time, Mr Winlock.'

'When?'

'At the earliest possible moment.'

'Can you tell me what it's about?'

'It's about a matter which concerns you personally, and which I think it would be unwise to discuss over the telephone even in general terms.'

'Where are you now?'

'I'm at the Mission Inn.'

'I have an important meeting a little later on, Mr Mason, but I can give you thirty minutes if you could come out right away.'

'I'll be there within ten minutes,' Mason promised.

'Thank you. Do you know where I live?'

'I have the address,' Mason said. 'I'll rely on a cab driver to get me there.'

Mason hung up the telephone, said to Della Street, 'You're going to have to hold the fort, Della. Keep in touch with things and I'll let you know as soon as I leave Winlock's.'

Nye said, 'I'll drive you out, Perry. I know where the place is. I can drive you out and wait until you finish your interview and drive you back.'

Mason hesitated a minute, then said, 'Okay, do that, if you will, Sid. It will save a few minutes and those few minutes may be precious. I want all the time I can have with Winlock.'

CHAPTER 8

GEORGE D. WINLOCK'S house was an imposing structure on a scenic knoll.

Nye parked the car in front of the door and said, 'I'll wait.'

'Okay,' Mason said. 'I shouldn't be very long.'

Mason ran up the steps to the porch, pressed the pearl button, heard the muted chimes in the interior of the house and almost instantly the door was opened by a young man in his late teens or early twenties who regarded Mason with insolent appraisal.

'Yeah?' he asked.

'I am Perry Mason,' the lawyer said. 'I have an appointment with George Winlock.'

'C'mon in,' the young man said.

Mason followed him into a reception hallway. The young man gestured towards a door on the right. 'George,' he yelled. 'C'mon down.'

He turned to Mason and said, 'Go on in there.'

Having said that, the young man turned his back, walked through a curtained doorway, and disappeared.

Mason went through the door indicated and found himself in a large room which was evidently used for entertaining purposes. In addition to the arrangement of chairs around the table in the centre of the room and in front of the fireplace, there were enough chairs along the sides to seat a dozen guests.

Mason was standing, looking around, when a tall, thin individual in the early fifties wearing dark glasses entered the room. He came forward with an air of quiet dignity, extended his hand, and said, 'How do you do, Mr Mason? I'm George Winlock.'

Mason shook hands and said, 'I'm sorry to disturb you outside of office hours but it is a matter which I considered to be of some importance.'

'I would certainly trust your judgement as to the importance of the matter,' Winlock said.

Mason studied the man thoughtfully. 'The matter is personal and it's rather embarrassing for me to bring it up.'

'Under those circumstances,' Winlock said, 'if you will be seated right here in this chair, Mr Mason, I'll take this one and we'll start right in without any preliminaries. I have an appointment later on and my experience has been that those things whch may prove embarrassing are best disposed of by going right to the heart of the matter and not beating around the bush.'

Mason said, 'Before seeking this interview, Mr Winlock, I tried to find out something about your background.'

'That,' Winlock said, 'would be simply a matter of good business judgement. I frequently do the same thing. If I am going to submit a proposition to someone, I like to know something about his background, his likes and dislikes.'

'And,' Mason went on, 'I found you had enjoyed a very successful career here in Riverside over the past fourteen years.'

Winlock merely inclined his head in a grave gesture of dignified assent.

'But,' Mason said, 'I couldn't find out anything at all about you before you came to Riverside.'

Winlock said quietly, 'I have been here for fourteen years, Mr Mason. I think that if you have any business matter to take up with me, you can certainly find out enough about me in connexion with my activities over that period to enable you to form a pretty good impression as to my likes and dislikes and my tastes.'

'That is quite true,' Mason said, 'but the matter that I have to take up with you is such that I would have liked to have known about your earlier background.'

'Perhaps if you'll tell me what the matter is,' Winlock said, 'it won't be necessary to take up so much of the limited time at our disposal searching into my background.'

'Very well,' Mason said. 'Do you know a Dianne Alder?'

'Alder, Alder,' Winlock said, pursing his lips thoughtfully. 'Now, it's difficult to answer that question, Mr Mason, because my business interests are very complex and I have quite an involved social life here. I don't have too good a memory

71

for names, offhand, and usually when a matter of that sort comes up I have to refer the inquiry to my secretary who keeps an alphabetical list of names that are important to me . . . May I ask if this person you mention, this Dianne Alder, is a client of yours?'

'She is,' Mason said.

'An interest which pivots about the affairs of some other client?' Winlock asked.

Mason laughed and said, 'Now you're cross-examining me, Mr Winlock.'

'Is there any reason why I shouldn't?'

'If you are not acquainted with Dianne Alder, there is no reason why you should,' Mason said.

'And if I am acquainted with this person?'

'Then,' Mason said, 'a great deal depends upon the nature of that knowledge – or, to put it another way, on the measure of the association.'

'Are you implying in any way that there has been an undue intimacy?' Winlock asked coldly.

'I am not implying any such thing,' Mason said. 'I am simply trying to get a plain answer to a simple question as to whether you know Dianne Alder.'

'I'm afraid I'm not in a position to answer that question definitely at the moment, Mason. I might be able to let you know later on.'

'Put it this way,' Mason said. 'The name means nothing to you at this time? You wouldn't know whether you were acquainted with her unless you had your secretary look it up on an alphabetical index?'

'I didn't exactly say that,' Winlock said. 'I told you generally something about my background in regard to people and names and then I asked you some questions which I consider very pertinent as to the nature and extent of your interest in ascertaining my knowledge, or lack of it, as far as the party in question is concerned.'

'All right,' Mason said, 'I'll stop sparring with you, Mr Winlock, and start putting cards on the table. Dianne Alder's father disappeared fourteen years ago. He was presumed to have been drowned. Now then, is there any possibility that prior to the time you came to Riverside there was a period in your life where you suffered from amnesia? Is it possible that, as a result of some injury or otherwise, you are not able to recall the circumstances of your life prior to arriving in Riverside? Is it possible that you could have had a family and perhaps a daughter and that your memory has become a blank as to such matters?

'Now, I am putting that in the form of a question, Mr Winlock. I am not making it as a statement, I am not making it as an accusation, I am not making it as a suggestion. I am simply putting it in the form of a question because I am interested in the answer. If the answer is no, then the interview is terminated as far as I am concerned.'

'You are acting upon the assumption that Dianne Alder may be my natural daughter?' Winlock asked.

'I am making no such statement, no such suggestion, and am acting upon no such assumption,' Mason said. 'I am simply asking you if, prior to the time you arrived in Riverside, there is any possibility that there is a hiatus in your memory due to amnesia, traumatic or otherwise.'

Winlock got to his feet. 'I'm sorry to disappoint you, Mr Mason, but there is no hiatus in my memory. I have never been bothered with amnesia and I remember my past life perfectly in all its details.

'I believe that answers your question and, as you remarked, an answer of this sort would terminate the interview as far as you are concerned.'

'That is quite correct,' Mason said, getting to his feet. 'I just wanted to be certain, that's all.'

'And may I ask why you came to me with this question?' Winlock asked, as he started escorting Mason to the door.

'Because,' Mason said, 'if there had been any possibility of such a situation existing, I might have been in a position to have spared you a great deal of embarrassment and trouble.'

'I see,' Winlock said, hesitating somewhat in his stride.

Mason stopped, faced the other man. 'One more question,' he said. 'Do you know a Harrison T. Boring who is at the moment registered in Unit 10 at the Restawhile Motel?'

'Boring ... Boring,' Winlock said, frowning. 'Now, there

73

again, Mr Mason, I'm going to have to point out to you that one of my pet peeves is having someone pull a name out of a hat and say, "Do you know this person or that person?" My business affairs are rather complex and—'

'I know, I know,' Mason interrupted, 'and your social life is not by any means simple. But if you know Harrison T. Boring in the way that you would know him if my surmise is correct, you wouldn't need to ask your secretary to look up his name on an alphabetical list.'

'And just what is your surmise, Mr Mason?'

'My surmise,' Mason said, 'is that regardless of whom he may be contacting, Harrison Boring tied Dianne Alder up in a contract by which he was in a position to collect a full fifty per cent of any gross income from any source whatever which Dianne might receive during the period of the next few years. He then dropped Dianne and repudiated the contract, indicating he had opened up a more lucrative market for any knowledge he might have.'

Winlock stood very stiff and very still. Then said, at length, 'You know that he made such a contract?'

'Yes.'

'May I ask the source of your information, Mr Mason?'

'I've seen the contract and know of its subsequent repudiation. If, therefore, you are not being frank with me, Mr Winlock, you should realize what the repudiation of Dianne's contract means. It means that Boring feels he could get *more* than half of what Dianne is entitled to. This means he has opened up a new source of income which he intends to use to the limit.'

'I think,' Winlock said, 'you had better come back here and sit down, Mr Mason. The situation is a little more complex than I had anticipated.'

Winlock walked back to the chair he had just vacated, seated himself, and indicated that Mason was to seat himself in the other chair.

Mason sat down and waited.

There was a long period of silence.

At length Mason took out his cigarette case, offered one to Winlock, who shook his head.

'Mind if *I* smoke?' Mason asked.

'Go right ahead. There's an ashtray there on the table.'

Mason lit the cigarette.

Winlock said, after a moment, 'What you have just told me, Mr Mason, is very much of a shock to me.'

Mason said nothing.

'All right,' Winlock said. 'I see that you are starting an investigation, Mr Mason, and I may as well forestall some of the results of that investigation. I had hoped that it never would be necessary for me to tell anyone the things I am going to tell you.

'My true name is George Alder. I was married to Eunice Alder. A little over fourteen years ago I started for Catalina Island in an open boat with an outboard motor. The boat ran out of fuel when we encountered head winds and heavy tide currents. We drifted about for a while, then a storm came up and the boat capsized. The accident happened at night. I am a good swimmer. I tried to keep in touch with my companion, but lost him in the darkness. I managed to keep myself afloat for some two hours. Then, as it was getting daylight, I saw a boat approaching. I managed to wave and shout and finally got the attention of one of the girls on the boat. She called out to the man at the wheel and the boat veered over and picked me up.

'I was near exhaustion.

'My married life had not been happy. My wife, Eunice, and I had, as it turned out, very little in common other than the first rush of passion which had brought about the marriage. When that wore off, and we settled down to a day-by-day relationship, we became mutually dissatisfied. She evidenced that dissatisfaction by finding fault with just about everything I did. If I drove a car, I was driving either too fast or too slow. If I reached a decision, she always questioned the decision.

'I evidenced my dissatisfaction by staying away from home a great deal and in the course of time developed other emotional interests.

'During the long hours I was swimming I felt that the situation was hopeless. I reviewed my past life. I realized that I should have separated from her while she was still young

75

enough to have attracted some other man. An attempt to sacrifice both our lives simply in order to furnish a home to a young daughter was, in my opinion, poor judgement.'

'It's difficult to judge a matter of that sort,' Mason said, 'because the judgement is usually made in connexion with the selfish interests of the person considering the situation.'

'Meaning that you don't agree with me?' Winlock said.

'Meaning that I was merely making a marginal comment,' Mason said. 'However, all that is in the past. If you want to justify your course of conduct I'm very glad to listen to you, but I feel that in view of what you have said we're getting to a point where time is short.'

'Exactly,' Winlock said. 'I'll put it this way. The boat that picked me up was headed for Catalina. I explained to them that I had been on a somewhat drunken party on another boat; that I had made a wager that I could swim to Catalina before the boat got there and had been drunk enough and foolish enough to plunge overboard to try it and the others had let me go, with a lot of jeering and facetious comments.

'I told my rescuers that I had a responsible position and that I certainly couldn't afford any publicity. So they fitted me out with clothes, which I agreed to return, and put me ashore at Catalina and said nothing about it.'

'Now then, recently Harrison T. Boring found out in some way what had happened and that I was actually George Alder.'

'And he has been asking money?'

'He has been paid money,' Winlock said. 'I gave him four separate payments, all of which represented blackmail. Boring came to Riverside in order to collect yet another payment. This time it was a very substantial payment and it was represented to me it would be a final payment.'

'How much?' Mason asked.

'Ten thousand dollars in cash,' Winlock said.

'Can you afford blackmail of that sort?' Mason asked.

'I can't afford not to pay blackmail. This man is in a position to wipe me out. Because I didn't dare to answer the questions in connexion with the vital statistics required on a marriage licence, I persuaded my present wife that there were

76

reasons why I didn't want to go through with another marriage and, because she was a divorced woman and the interlocutory degree had not become final, we simply announced to our friends that we had run away and had been married in Nevada over a weekend.

'I may state that at that time the circle of my friends was much more limited than is the case at the present time, and what we did – or rather, what we said we had done – attracted very little attention. There was, I believe, a small article in the society column of the local newspaper.'

'But how do you feel about Dianne?' Mason asked. 'You simply walked out of her life. You deprived her of a father, you never let her know—'

'I *couldn't* let her know,' Winlock said. 'I had to make a clean break. There was no other way out of it. However, I may state that I have kept in touch with Dianne without her knowing anything at all about it. If she ever had any real need for money, I'd have seen that she had it.

'She had a very good job as a secretary with Corning, Chester, and Corning of Bolero Beach. She has perhaps no realization of just how she secured that job. If it hadn't been for the influence of a firm of attorneys here in Riverside, who, in turn, were indebted to me, I doubt very much that Dianne would have secured such a good job so early in her career.

'However, that's neither here nor there. I am not trying to justify myself to you, Mr Mason, I am simply pointing out that your statement to me is a great shock, because it is now apparent that Boring is not interested in a lump sum settlement as he told me, but plans to bleed me white.

'This would kill my wife. To have a scandal come out at this particular time, to have it appear our relationship was illicit, to lose her social prestige— Well, I can't even bear to think of it.'

'Your wife has a son by another marriage?'

'That's right. And as far as he is concerned, I— Well, I am not talking about him. If something happened that would— If that young man had to go out and stand on his two feet— Oh, well, that's neither here nor there. There's no use discussing it.'

Mason said, 'May I ask what Boring told you when he solicited this last ten-thousand-dollar cash payment?'

Winlock shrugged his shoulders. 'Probably it would be an old story to you,' he said. 'The man rang me up. He told me that he was sincerely repentant; that he was just being a common blackmailer; that it was ruining his character and making a crook and a sneak of him; that he had an opportunity to engage in legitimate business; that he needed ten thousand dollars as operating capital; that if he could get this one lump sum, he could invest it in such a way that he could have an assured income and that I would never hear from him again.

'He promised me that if I got him this one ten-thousand-dollar payment, that that would be the last; that he would, as he expressed it, go straight from that point on. That I would have the satisfaction of knowing I had straightened him out at the same time that I was relieving myself of the possibility of any further payments.'

'You believed him?' Mason asked.

'I paid him the ten thousand dollars,' Winlock said dryly. 'I had no choice in the matter.'

'The line of patter Boring handed you,' Mason said, 'is just about standard with a certain type of blackmailer.'

'What are *you* going to do?' Winlock asked.

'I don't know,' Mason told him. 'Remember, I am representing your daughter, but that she has no suspicion of the true facts in the case – as yet. As her attorney, I will tell her. Now, what do *you* intend to do?'

'There is only one thing I can do,' Winlock said. 'I must throw myself on Dianne's mercy. I must ask her to accept financial restitution and leave my wife with her social position intact. That would be all I could hope for.'

'But if you could come to terms with Dianne, what are you going to do about Boring?' Mason asked.

Winlock's shoulders slumped. 'I wish I knew,' he said simply. 'And now, Mr Mason, I simply *must* keep my other appointment.'

Mason shook hands. 'I'm sorry to bring you bad news.'

'I had it coming,' Winlock said, and escorted him to the door.

'Situation coming to a head?' Sid Nye asked, as Mason opened the door and jumped in the car beside him.

'The situation is coming to a boil,' Mason said, 'and I think it's going to be advantageous to take some further steps in the interests of justice.'

'Such as what?' Nye asked.

'Such as scaring the living hell out of a blackmailer,' Mason told him. 'Let's go to the hotel. We'll talk with Paul Drake, find out if he knows anything, get in touch with Della Street, and then set the stage for one hell of a fight.'

Nye grinned. 'I take it your interview with Winlock was satisfactory?'

'It opened up possibilities,' Mason said.

Nye said, 'A kid went tearing out of here in a sports car seven or eight minutes ago, and a dame who is a knockout drove out just a minute or two ago. That mean anything?'

Mason was thoughtful as Nye started the automobile. 'I think it does,' he said at length.

CHAPTER 9

SID NYE drove Mason to the Mission Inn, said, 'Well, I'll go on about my business, Perry, and check up on what's happening. I'll keep in touch with you. You're going to be at the hotel?'

'As far as I know,' Mason told him.

'Okay, I'll do a little checking. If you need me, you can get me at the Tri-Counties Detective Agency. I'll be there.'

'Okay, thanks a lot,' Mason said. He watched Nye drive away, then entered the hotel and went up to his suite.

'Well, Della,' he asked, 'how about dinner?'

'I was hoping you'd think of that,' she said, 'but I have news for you.'

'What?'

'Dianne is here.'

'Where?'

'Somewhere in Riverside. I told her she'd better come up here and wait for you but she was all worked up.'

'What did she want?'

'Montrose Foster has been in touch with her all right.'

'And upset her?'

'I'll say it upset her. He told her the facts of life.'

'Such as what?'

'That Boring was only trying to get something out of her for his own good. He asked her if Boring had got her to sign anything, and she said he had, and he wanted to see the contract but she didn't give him any satisfaction.'

'Then what?'

'Then Foster started trying to pump her about her family, trying to find out something on which he could capitalize and trying to keep Dianne in the dark. You'll never guess the one he finally lit on.'

'What?'

'The good old stand-by,' Della Street said. 'White slavery. Dianne has read enough about that and seen enough about it in Hollywood pictures so she fell for it, hook, line, and sinker. Foster told her that Boring was just grooming her for immoral purposes, that before he got done with her he'd have her where she couldn't fight back, and that she'd wind up as a dope fiend, a physical, moral wreck. He told her that whatever contract she signed it was entered into under false pretences; that Boring was a fly-by-night; that he was strictly no good; that he was an opportunist; that he'd get her to give up her job, lose contact with her friends; get her in his power with a few hundred dollars and then lower the boom.'

'And Dianne fell for it?'

'She's so upset she hardly knows what she's doing. She didn't tell him about Boring terminating the contract.'

'How did she know that we were here?'

'That apparently was more or less of an accident. She came here on her own and heard someone talking in the lobby about Perry Mason, the attorney, being registered here in the hotel. So she telephoned from a drugstore.'

'But why did she come to Riverside in the first place, Della?'

'She knows Boring is here. She asked me if I thought she should confront him and demand an explanation. She said she wanted to let him know he'd have to give her back that copy of the contract he had with her signature on it. She is so worked up now she seems to think that the contract is an agreement to fatten herself up and go to South America to lead an immoral life. The poor kid is hysterical. I tried to talk to her but she wouldn't let the words get through. I told her to come here at once.'

'Did she say she would?'

'She didn't say anything except what a mess she'd be in if Boring let anyone know she'd signed a contract to become a quote white slave unquote.'

'Well,' Mason said, 'under the circumstances, I think we should stay here in the suite until Dianne shows up. Did she tell Foster anything about her father?'

'Apparently,' Della Street said, 'Foster is overlooking the obvious. He was trying to get Dianne to talk about her family, about her father's brothers and sisters, about her mother's relatives. He's looking for some distant tie-in, some obscure relative she has lost track of who could have died and left her a fortune that no one knows about.

'How did you come out with Winlock? Any luck?'

'We hit pay dirt, Della.'

'Then, Dianne is his daughter?'

'Yes. She's his daughter and she's a blackmailer's bonanza.'

'What are you going to do?' she asked.

'Throw some of *my* weight around,' Mason said. 'I have three objectives. First, to safeguard Dianne's interests; second, to keep Foster from finding out the facts; third, to scare the living hell out of a blackmailer so he'll become a fugitive from justice.'

'And then what?' Della Street asked.

'Boring has taken ten thousand dollars blackmail money. I don't know whether we can prove it so it will stand up in court, but he undoubtedly has the ten thousand dollars in cash in his possession. He can't explain how he got it.

'Winlock is sitting on the edge of a volcano. I don't know just what he's worth but I imagine we can make a deal with him by which Dianne can get at least a half million dollars in return for not blowing the whistle – but before we make any settlement with Winlock, we'll find out just how much is involved. I think when Dianne knows the facts, she'll be inclined to be charitable, but there's the emotional shock which has to be cushioned.'

'When will she know the facts?' Della Street asked.

'Just as soon as I see her,' Mason said. 'She's my client. I'm her attorney. My knowledge is her knowledge. I can tell her what I know in confidence and then we'll work out the best course of action, but I have her emotions to consider.'

'We were,' Della Street reminded him, 'talking about dinner.'

'I think they have excellent room service here,' Mason said. 'We'll have a big porterhouse steak, with baked potatoes and sour cream, tomato and avocado salad, Thousand Island dressing, and—'

'Heavens!' Della Street said. 'Are you trying to make a Dianne Alder out of me? Am *I* supposed to put on twelve pounds?'

Mason said, 'You're working for a fiend in human form. I'm fattening you up for the South American market.'

'My resistance has turned to putty,' Della Street said. 'I'm unable to resist the thought of savoury food ... Suppose Dianne comes in while we're waiting or while we're eating?'

'That's the idea of the big porterhouse steak,' Mason said. 'We'll have it big enough so we can put in an extra plate and feed Dianne.'

'If you're going to feed her,' Della Street said, 'you'd better order a double chocolate malted milk and some mince pie alamode on the side.'

'And if Dianne shouldn't show up?' Mason asked. 'I suppose you could—'

Della Street threw up her hands. 'Don't do it,' she said. 'I might not be able to resist.'

Mason looked at his watch. 'Well,' he said, 'I think Dianne will probably be in. Ring the registration desk and see if she's here or has a reservation, Della, and get room service and have the food sent up here in forty-five minutes.'

Della Street inquired for Dianne Alder, found out that she was not registered at the hotel, contacted room service, and ordered the meal.

While they were waiting, Mason put through a call to Paul Drake. 'Anything new at your end, Paul?'

'Things have simmered down here.'

'Dianne is up here,' Mason said. 'Sit right there in your office. Things are coming to a head. You can have some hamburgers sent in.'

'Have a heart, Perry. I was taking soda bicarbonate all afternoon.'

'Well,' Mason said, 'on second thought, Paul, you may as well go out, but be back inside an hour and leave word with the office where you can be reached. I've seen Winlock and now I know all the answers.'

'You mean he admitted—'

'I mean we're okay,' Mason said, 'but I can't discuss it.'

'How long do you want my men on the job up there, Perry?'

'Until I tell you to quit. I think we're about at the end of the case now – at least this phase of it – but our friend, Dillard, is anchored there at the motel. Evidently Boring has him spotted and is getting pretty suspicious.'

'What are you going to do with Boring?'

'After I've seen Dianne,' Mason said, 'I'm going down and have a heart-to-heart talk with Boring.'

'You mean the party is going to get rough?'

'I mean the party is going to get *very* rough.'

'Can you handle him, Perry?'

'I can handle him. I never saw any blackmailer yet I couldn't handle. I'm going to put him in such a position that he'll consider himself a fugitive from justice, and if his conscience makes him resort to flight and concealment of his identity, I don't see how I can be expected to do anything about that.'

'Certainly not,' Drake said. 'You'll be a paragon of righteous virtue. I'm on my way, Perry. I'll leave word in the office where I can be reached, but don't call me until I've wrapped myself around the outside of a steak and French fried potatoes.'

'Better make it a baked potato,' Mason said, 'or you'll be eating bicarbonate again. Be good, Paul.'

The lawyer hung up, looked at his watch, said, 'I wish Dianne would show up. I want to have *all* the reins in my hand before I start driving.'

It was, however, twenty minutes later that there was a timid knock at the door of the suite.

Mason nodded to Della Street. 'Dianne,' he said.

Della went over and opened the door.

Dianne Alder stood on the threshold.

'Come in, Dianne,' Della Street said. 'He's here.'

Dianne followed her into the room, gave Mason a forced smile, said, 'Oh, I'm so glad.'

'Sit down,' Mason said. 'We have a nice steak coming up and you look to me as though you could use a drink.'

'I could use two of them,' she said.

'All in, eh?' Mason asked.

She nodded.

Mason said, 'Look, Dianne, let's get certain things straightened out. You've paid me a retainer. I'm your attorney. We have a confidential relationship. Anything you tell me is in confidence; anything that I learn which could affect you in any way, I tell you. I'm obligated to. Do you understand?'

'Yes.'

'Now, you're in for a shock,' Mason told her. 'You're going to have some information which is going to hit you right where you live ... What do you want to drink?'

'Is brandy all right?'

'No,' Mason said. 'That's not the kind of a before-dinner drink you should have – you want a Manhattan or a Martini.'

'I don't think I want anything to eat.'

Mason said, 'What's the matter, Dianne? Something seems to be bothering you. Suppose you start by telling me a few things. Why did you come to Riverside in such a rush?'

'I ... I wanted to see somebody.'

'Who?'

'Mr Boring.'

'You knew he was up here?'

'Yes.'

'How did you know?'

'Someone told me.'

'Who?'

'A man who knows him very well. Someone he used to work for.'

'Montrose Foster?'

'Yes.'

'What else did Foster tell you?'

'That I've been a little fool, that Mr Boring was just trying to take advantage of me and that the contract about using me for a model was all just eyewash; that what he really had in mind was something altogether different.'

Mason regarded her thoughtfully, said, 'Did he tell you what it was, Dianne?'

'White slavery.'

Mason crossed over and put a hand on her shoulder. 'Look, Dianne,' he said, 'this has been a rough day as far as you're concerned. You've had some shocks and you're going to have some more shocks. You've been seeing too many movies. Now quit worrying about Boring. Leave him to me.'

The telephone rang.

Mason nodded to Della Street, again turned to Dianne. 'Look, Dianne, you're shaking like a leaf. What's the trouble?'

She started to cry.

Della Street, on the telephone, said, 'I'll get him right away, Sid.'

She nodded to Mason. 'Sid Nye. Says it's important.'

Mason hurried across to the telephone, picked up the instrument, said, 'Yes, Sid. What is it?'

'I don't know,' Nye said, 'but I've had a call from Moose Dillard. It was a peculiar call.'

'What was it?'

'He said, "Sid, do you know who is talking?" and I recognized his voice and said yes, and he said, "Hey Rube" and hung up.'

'Just that?' Mason asked.

'Just that. Just *Hey Rube*. He worked for a circus at one time. You can figure what that means.'

'Where are you now?'

'At the Tri-Counties.'

'How long will it take you to get down to the front of the Mission Inn?'

'About two minutes.'

'I'll be there,' Mason said.

The lawyer hung up the telephone, turned to Della Street. 'Della,' he said, 'tell Dianne the story. Break it to her easy, one woman to another. When the food comes up, give her some food and put a piece of steak aside for me. I may be back in time to get it. I may not.'

'Two Martinis for Dianne?' Della Street asked.

Mason shifted his eyes to Dianne.

She met his gaze for a moment, then lowered her eyes.

Mason whirled to Della Street. 'Not a damn one,' he said, 'and she's not to talk with anyone until I get back. Understand? Not anyone!'

Mason made a dash for the door.

CHAPTER 10

SID NYE picked Mason up in front of the Mission Inn.

'What do you make of it, Sid?'

'It's a jam of some sort. Moose isn't one to lose his head in a situation of that kind. Evidently something's happened and he didn't dare say anything over the phone because the call probably went through the switchboard at the motel. He evidently wanted to use something that I'd understand and other people wouldn't. Moose is quite a character. He had a circus background and he knew I'd understand Hey Rube.'

'That means a free-for-all fight?' Mason asked.

'Not exactly. It means that all the carnival people gather

together against the outsiders. It may or may not mean a clem, but it means you start knocking anything or anybody out of your way and — well, it's just a good old rallying battle cry.'

Nye was piloting the car with deft skill through the traffic. 'Then Dillard needs help?'

'He sure as hell does,' Nye said. 'It could be almost anything. It means he's in a hell of a jam and wants us to get there.'

'Well,' Mason said, 'it suits me all right. I'm due to have a little talk with Harrison T. Boring as of now.'

'It's a talk he'll like?' Nye asked, grinning.

Mason said, 'It's a talk which will, I hope, give Mr Boring an entirely new series of ideas and perhaps a complete change of environment.'

Nye swung the car down a side street, suddenly slowed, said, 'That's a police car in front of the place, Perry.'

'What number is Dillard in?' Mason asked.

'Number 5.'

'All right,' Mason said, 'drive right up to Number 5. If Dillard is in trouble we'll be right there. If the police car is there for someone else, we'll pay no attention but go into Dillard's place.'

Nye swung into the entrance of the motel, found a parking place, switched off headlights and ignition, looked to Mason for instructions.

'Right into Number 5,' Mason said.

The lawyer and Nye converged on the door of Number 5.

'Try the knob,' Mason said in an undertone.

Nye was reaching for the knob when the door opened.

There were no lights on inside the unit. The big lumbering individual who hulked in the doorway said in a husky voice, 'Come on in.'

'No lights?' Nye asked.

'No lights,' Dillard said, and closed the door behind them. 'Don't stumble over anything. Your eyes'll get accustomed to the darkness in a minute. I'm sitting here at the window with the curtains parted so I can get a line on what's happening.'

'What is happening?'

87

'I don't know. The police are there now, and the ambulance left just a few minutes ago.'

'The ambulance?' Nye said.

'That's right. They took him away.'

'Who? Boring?'

'Right.'

Nye said, 'You know Perry Mason, Moose.'

'Sure,' Moose said, his hand groping for Mason's in the dark. 'How are you, Mr Mason? Haven't seen you for a while.'

Then he said, by way of explanation to Nye, 'Mason got me out of a jam a while back.'

'I know,' Nye said. 'Just wanted to be sure you recognized him in the dark. Now, what's been happening out here?'

'Plenty has been happening,' Dillard said, 'but what it's all about is more than I know. Boring was having a convention. All sorts of people coming and going. Then the girl showed up and left in a hurry and about ten minutes after she left the cops came. I wanted to keep casing the joint and didn't want to give a tip-off to the manager. I had a hell of a time getting anyone on the phone. Whatever was happening, it took their attention off the switchboard. Finally I managed to get them to answer – you can't get an outside line on these phones unless they connect you – I guess I was all of five minutes jiggling that hook up and down, putting the light on and off, waiting for someone to answer.'

'All right,' Nye said, 'they answered. Was there anything unusual? Did they apologize or make any explanation?'

'Not a word. Someone said, "Manager's office", and I said, "I want to get an outside line", and the manager said, "You can't dial a number from this phone. You have to give me the number and I connect you." So I gave them the number of the Tri-Counties and asked for you. I was pretty certain they were listening on the line. I could hear breathing. So I just told you, "Hey Rube", and hung up. I figured that would get you here as quick as anything and I didn't want to ask you to come rushing out because I knew you'd ask questions and if I started answering questions we'd have this unit under surveillance and that might not be the thing you wanted.'

'That's good thinking,' Mason said. 'What happened after that?'

'An ambulance came right after I hung up. They took him out on a stretcher.'

'He isn't dead then,' Mason said.

'It was an ambulance, not a meat wagon. I don't know what sort of a system they use here but I have an idea the ambulance means the guy's hurt.'

'All right,' Mason said, 'let's find out what happened. Who came here?'

'I can't give you names,' Dillard said. 'I can give you one licence number and some descriptions. That's all I have to go on at the present time.'

'You were watching through the window?'

'Had the lights out and the curtains parted and a pair of eyeglass binoculars. Those have about a two and a half power magnification; and then I've got an eight-power binocular here that is a night glass. I use it on surveillance jobs of this sort.'

'All right, what can you give us?' Mason asked.

'I can't give you too much without turning the light on so I can read my notes. I made the notes in the dark.'

'Tell us what you can remember.'

'First rattle out of the box,' Dillard said, 'there was this fellow who's been prowling around Bolero Beach; a slim, fast-moving guy with a mosquito beak for a nose ...'

'His name's Montrose Foster,' Mason said. 'He's the president, whatever that means, of Missing Heirs and Lost Estates, Inc. Boring was working for him until he suddenly quit his job, and Foster thinks Boring hit some pay dirt that he didn't want to share with anyone.'

'Could be,' Dillard said. 'Anyway, this fellow came in around eight and he was there about fifteen minutes. I've got the times marked down.'

'Now, you could see all of these people all right?' Mason asked.

'Sure. There was some daylight when this man you call Foster was here. And later on there's enough light here in the parking place so I could see people well enough to identify them.'

'Okay,' Mason said. 'Then what happened?'

'Well, for about five minutes after this man Foster left there was nothing doing. I kept thinking our man would go out to dinner but he didn't. He seemed to be waiting for someone or something. And then, around twenty minutes past eight, this kid driving a sports car showed up and boy, was he making time! He slammed that sports car into the entrance and wham! right up to Unit Number 10. He jumped out and was inside all in one motion. It was getting dark then.'

'Did he knock on the door?' Mason asked.

'He knocked.'

'How old was this man?'

'Around twenty-two to twenty-three; somewhere in there; driving a high-powered foreign sports model. He parked it at such an angle I couldn't get the licence number.'

'On a guess,' Mason said, 'that was Marvin Harvey Palmer.

'All right, how long did he stay?'

'Somewhere around fifteen minutes. Then he left and a woman came in, a woman about forty, and boy, was she worked up! She went in the minute the kid went out. She was just as stately as you please, and she was in there nearly ten minutes. Then she came out, and that's when the man went in. Now, this man had been waiting. He'd seen the woman's car and recognized it, or had seen the woman or something; anyway, he'd parked his car down at the far end of the parking place here, then he'd seen the woman's car and he'd driven out, parked his car in the street someplace, and walked in and hung around in the shadows down at the far end waiting for the woman to leave. He was a dignified guy wearing dark glasses. The minute the woman left he hot-footed it across to Unit 10, banged on the door, and went in and was there about five minutes. He came out and things simmered down for about ten minutes and then this blonde came in and boy, was she a knockout ... I got the licence number on *her* car.'

'Did you get a good look at her?' Mason asked.

'I'll say I got a good look at her. She parked the car and opened the door on the left-hand side and slid out from behind the steering wheel. Believe me she was in a hurry and she didn't care how she looked when she got out – she was just getting out.

'Unit 10 was on the other side of the car from her and when she opened the door and slid out she was coming right towards me. Her skirt just rolled up under her and – boy, oh, boy, talk about legs!'

'Let's go a little higher than the legs,' Mason said. 'What about her face?'

'Around twenty-four or so; blonde, tall, and my God, what a figure! She really filled out her clothes.'

'All right,' Mason said, 'this is important. Now, what time did she go in and how long was she in there?'

'She went in about ten minutes after the man left and she was in there, I guess, ten or fifteen minutes. And when she came out she was all excited. Boy, was *she* running! She made a dive for her car. This time she went in the door that was on the right-hand side and slid across the seat. She threw the car into reverse and whipped out of here in such a hurry that she forgot to turn her headlights on. I've got the time written down in my notebook.'

'And after that?' Mason asked.

'After that, everything was quiet for a couple of minutes. Then the manager came down and pounded on the door and after a while opened the door and went in. Then she came out on the run and a few minutes after that the police came.'

'All right,' Mason said. 'Now, let's get this straight. You have been watching this place ever since – what time?'

'Ever since the guy got in here, or right after he got in.'

'You know every person who went into that motel. You saw everyone.'

'Sure, I saw them.'

'There's no back entrance?'

'Just the one door. That is, we may have to check it, but I'm sure there's just one door because that's the way the places are laid out ... and Sid was going to send someone in with some eats for me ... Boy, I'm famished!'

'Never mind that,' Mason said. 'This blonde was in there for how long?'

'About fifteen minutes.'

'And she was the last one in?'

'That's right. This guy was hurt. If it was a fist fight, it was the man. If it was a shot or a stab, it could have been the girl – probably was, because she was the last one in.'

Mason took Nye to one side, said in a low voice, 'We'll peg the first man definitely as Montrose Foster. We'll peg the next man tentatively as Marvin Harvey Palmer, and the third visitor could have been Mrs Winlock. Then the man with the dark glasses we can be pretty certain was George Winlock ... What time did we leave the Winlock residence, Sid?'

'Right around eight twenty-five,' Nye said.

'And it's how far from the Winlock residence here?'

'Not over five minutes if you're driving in a hurry. Both the motel here and the Winlock residence are on the same side of town.'

'All right,' Mason said. 'As soon as we left the place, George Winlock jumped in his automobile and drove here. He found his wife's car parked out in front.

'Now, if that second visitor was Marvin Harvey Palmer, he must have left the house to come out here a short time *before* we left the house. You told me a sports car left the place.'

Nye said, 'Would it be in order to ask if your interview with Goerge Winlock exploded a bombshell?'

'It exploded a bombshell,' Mason said.

'All right,' Nye said, 'the answer is simple. The room was bugged. The kid found out what was going on and wanted to beat everybody to the punch, so he came tearing out here.'

'Then what happened?' Mason asked.

'Then the wife followed. She was ready to start at about the same time but she wanted to put on her face and take the shine off her nose.

'Her husband left immediately after we did. He drove out here and – well, that's it.'

They moved over to join Dillard.

'Whatever happened,' Dillard repeated, 'is the result of what the blonde did.'

'Now, wait a minute,' Mason told him. 'You're getting out of orbit, Dillard. The blonde in all probability is my client.'

'Oh-oh,' Dillard said.

'It's one thing for you to say what time she came and what time she left,' Mason went on, 'but it's quite another thing to have you making any big fat surmises as to what happened while she was in that cabin.'

'I'm sorry,' Dillard apologized, 'I guess I spoke out of turn, but – well, the way I looked at it, there was no other way of figuring it.'

'There may be another way of looking at it,' Mason said. 'Let's suppose that this young man tried to get something from Boring and got a little rough. He left Boring lying unconscious on the floor. The woman could have been the boy's mother. She went in and found the man lying on the floor, dying. She also found some weapon that tied the crime in with her son. She paused long enough to straighten certain things up, remove certain bits of evidence, including the weapon; then she took off.

'The man could have been her husband. He was waiting for her to come out so he could go in. He'd spotted her car as soon as he drove up.'

'And the minute he spotted the car,' Nye said, 'he knew that the room in his house had been bugged and that his wife had been listening in on whatever conversation it was that you had with him.'

'Well,' Mason said, 'let's suppose that the boy *had* hit Boring with the butt of a revolver, and that his mother found Boring unconscious and got out; then the husband, coming in as soon as his wife had left, found the man in a dying condition. He looked around just long enough to make certain his wife hadn't left any clues that would indicate she had been there – that meant *he* could have been the one who picked up the revolver – and then *he* got out.'

Dillard asked, 'Have you fellows got names to put on these tags of son, mother, and husband?'

'We *think* we have,' Mason said. 'I'm talking in terms of tags instead of names because you're going to be a witness. If you haven't heard any names, it'll be that much better for you.'

Dillard said, 'You fellows figure it up any way you want to. All I know is that the blonde was the last one in the room. If she's your client, I'm not going to start guessing what she was doing in there for fifteen minutes, but you know what the police are going to think. You may sell your idea to a jury, but the police won't buy it. They'll feel that if she found the man lying on the floor badly injured or dying, she wouldn't have stuck around for fifteen minutes.'

Nye said, 'Let me ask you a straight question, Dillard. Do you ever lose pages out of your notebook?'

'Not in a murder case,' Dillard said. 'I've been in enough trouble.'

'You have, for a fact,' Mason told him.

'But,' Dillard went on, 'I don't have to tell *all* I know if I haven't anyone to tell it to.'

'What do you mean?'

'I could be hard to find.'

Mason thought things over and said, 'I don't think that's the answer, Dillard.'

'Well, what is the answer?' Dillard asked.

'I'll be darned if I know,' Mason said, 'but I've got to talk with my client before the police talk with her and before the police get wise to you.'

'Well, you've got to move plenty fast,' Dillard said, 'because the police are going to get wise to me.'

'How do you figure that out?'

'I checked in here right after Boring. I got the place across the parking lot where I could have a good view of his unit.'

'You say you got it?' Mason asked.

'That's right.'

'How did you get it?'

'I asked for it.'

'Oh-oh,' Nye said. 'That *is* going to put the fat in the fire.'

'Why did you ask for it?' Mason inquired.

'Because I didn't want to sit out there in my car. That's too damn conspicuous. I wanted a place where I could look across the parking place. I asked the manager what she had and she told me she had several vacancies and I asked for Number 5. I asked if it was vacant and she said it was and I said I wanted it.'

'Did she ask you why?'

'She didn't *ask* anything but she looked me over a couple of

94

times and once she begins to put two and two together, she's going to tell the police about me. They'll ask her if there was anything unusual and she'll say no, and then they'll ask her about other tenants and if anybody checked in about the same time that Boring did, or a little after he did, and then she'll remember me and then the police will start talking to me if I'm around. Or, if I'm not around, they'll check the registration card for the licence number on the automobile, find it's in the name of Paul Drake, and then they'll want to see me.'

Mason said to Nye, 'I've got to go talk with my client right away. Dillard, you can sit here in the dark and I'll give you a ring if I need to.'

'Remember one thing,' Dillard told him. 'If you should give me a ring *after* the police have asked questions of the manager, somebody will be listening in on the line.'

Mason said, 'I usually act on the assumption someone *is* listening in on the line.'

'If I don't hear from you, then what?' Dillard asked.

'Get out as best you can,' Mason said. 'On second thoughts, it might be a good plan to get out of here right now ... You haven't had any supper?'

'That's right. They said a dame would bring me some sandwiches.'

Nye snapped his fingers. 'I've got to contact the agency and head her off. If she should come walking in here right now, it *would* cause trouble.'

'Why not go get something to eat?' Mason asked Dillard. 'There's no use keeping Unit 10 under surveillance now. The police will have it blocked off and probably will have a detective spending the night in there, just to see if any telephone calls come in.'

'Okay,' Dillard said, 'I'll go to dinner.'

'We'll go out together,' Nye said. 'I'll take Mason to the hotel and come back and get you.'

'I have my car here, you know,' Dillard said.

'Then we'll take both cars,' Nye told him. 'I'll take Mason to the hotel and I'll have to head off that woman operative with the sandwiches and coffee.'

Mason nodded. 'On our way, Sid.'

CHAPTER 11

DELLA STREET said, 'We saved it for you, Chief, but it's all cold. I didn't dare to keep it in the warming oven for fear it would be too well done.'

'That's all right,' Mason said. 'I'll eat it cold.'

'Oh, no,' Della Street protested. 'Let's have another hot one sent up. I'll—'

'There may not be time,' Mason said. 'You didn't eat much, Dianne.'

'I didn't— Somehow I don't seem to be hungry.'

'A little different from the way you were when I first met you,' Mason said.

'Yes, I—'

'Something happened to change the picture?' Mason asked conversationally, seating himself and cutting off a piece of the steak. 'You don't crave food as you feared you would?'

'I . . . I don't know. I guess I just lost my appetite.'

'What did you come up here for?' Mason asked.

'To Riverside?'

'Yes.'

'To see Mr Boring.'

'See him?'

'Not yet. Della said to come here. I know now after listening to her, that you should be the one to do the talking.'

There was silence for a minute.

Della Street said, 'The coffee is hot, Chief. I kept that going over the candle flame but it isn't fresh – it will only take a few minutes to get more coffee.'

Mason shook his head, said to Dianne, 'Right now Boring is either at the hospital or at the morgue.'

'Why?' she asked, her eyes wide. 'Did something happen to him?'

'Something happened to him,' Mason said.

Dianne put her hand to her throat. Her eyes got large and round.

'Something happened to him,' Mason said, 'while you were talking with him.'

'I ... I ...' She started, blinking back tears.

Mason said, 'Now look, Dianne. You're playing a dangerous game. It can possibly trap you into a life term in a prison cell. You can't afford to lie to your lawyer. Now, tell me the truth. What happened?'

'What do you mean, what happened?'

Mason said, 'You went to the Restawhile Motel. You knew that Boring was in Unit 10. You called on him. Now, did you find him lying on the floor or—'

'Lying on the floor!' she exclaimed. 'What do you mean?'

'Go on,' Mason said. 'Tell me the truth. And don't ever lie to me – don't ever try to lie to me again, Dianne. If you do, I'm going to walk out on you.'

She said, 'All right, Mr Mason, I'll tell you the truth. I wanted to tell you the truth all along. I *did* see him. I knew he was up here at the Restawhile.'

'Who told you?'

'This man that told me so much about him. He told me where I could find him. He told me that the only thing to do was to make him give me back the other copy of that contract; that he had deliberately tricked me and that he didn't care a thing in the world about whether I put on one pound or fifty; that all of that stuff about being a model and building up my figure and all that was just so much eyewash, that he would use that contract to get me to go to South America and then suddenly cut me off without any funds and I'd have to ... to sell myself. He said that as long as Boring had that contract with my name on it, he could ruin my reputation any time he wanted to.'

'Did you tell him Boring had terminated that contract?' Mason asked.

'No, because I felt that so-called repudiation was just a part of the plan to get me in his power.'

'What time did you see Boring?' Mason asked.

'Just before I came here.'

'And did he tear up the contract?'

'He ... gave it back to me.'

97

'And then what?'

'Then I walked out.'

'How long were you there?'

'The whole thing couldn't have been over five minutes.'

'And when you left, what about it?'

'Then I came here.'

'How long were you in there?'

'It couldn't have been – not over five minutes.'

'You couldn't have been in there fifteen or twenty minutes?'

'Heavens, no, Mr Mason. I don't think I was in there five minutes. Those things happen awfully fast. I don't think I was in there over two minutes. I just told him that I'd found out about him and found out about that contract and it was all a phony and I wanted to call things off and I wanted him to give me that other copy of the contract back.'

'And then what?'

'And then he said that he didn't know who had been talking to me but he had my name on the dotted line and, as he said, he had me sewed up.'

'And then what?'

'Mr Mason, I've been over it. It's just the way I told you. He told me that he had me all sewed up and I told him that I knew he was a big phony, that the whole contract was a phony, that he didn't have any career as a model for me, that he just wanted to get me in his power, and he laughed and said I *was* in his power, and I told him I wasn't, that if he thought he could make me do anything that wasn't right just because of the money involved, he had two more guesses coming and that I had retained you as my lawyer and then he gave me the contract. That scared him.'

Mason said, 'Look, Dianne, this can be very, very serious. If you picked up a chair and clubbed him over the head while you were defending yourself, or if you used a weapon or if he tumbled and fell, all you have to do is to say so. You've got a good reputation, you can create a good impression and a jury will believe you. But if you try to tell a lie and get caught, it's going to mean you're going to be convicted of homicide; perhaps manslaughter, perhaps even second-degree murder.'

She tried to meet his eyes but failed.

'Dianne,' Mason said, 'you're lying.'

Abruptly she said, 'I *have* to lie, Mr Mason. The truth is simply too utterly devastating.'

Mason said harshly, 'You've wasted enough time trying to lie. You can't get away with it, Dianne. You're an amateur. You're not a good enough liar. You haven't had enough practice. Now, tell me the truth before it's too late.'

'What do you mean, too late?'

'The police,' Mason said. 'They may be here any minute. Now, tell me the truth.'

'I'm afraid you won't believe me.'

'Tell me the truth,' Mason said, 'and get started – fast!'

'All right,' she said, 'I went to the motel unit and – well, I was all worked up and excited and indignant and—'

'Never mind all that,' Mason said. 'What did you do?'

'I went to the door and it was open just an inch or two and I could see a light on inside. I knocked and no one answered so I pushed the door open and – well, there he was, lying on the floor. The place reeked with the smell of whisky and I thought he was dead drunk.'

'You didn't hit him with anything?'

She shook her head vehemently. 'Heavens, no! He was lying there. I thought he was drunk and so I looked around to try and find his signed copy of my contract.'

'And you found it?'

'Yes.'

'Where?'

'In a briefcase.'

'You took it?'

'Yes.'

'Then what?'

'I bent over him and it was then I noticed that he was hurt. The whisky wasn't on his breath, it was on his clothes.'

'Then what?'

'I ran out, drove to a phone booth about three blocks down the street, called the office of the motel, told the woman who answered that the man in Unit Number 10 had been hurt, and then hung up the phone before she could ask any questions.

'Then I came up here.'

'Dianne,' Mason said, 'you're still lying. You had to make quite a search to find that contract. You found Boring unconscious on the floor. You started looking through his baggage and through his clothes, trying to find that contract. You didn't find it until nearly fifteen minutes had passed, and you found ten thousand dollars in money and you took that along with the contract.'

She shook her head. 'It was just as I told you. I took the contract. I didn't see any money.'

'How long were you in there?'

'I don't think it was two minutes.'

'Then why did you try to lie to me at first?'

'I was afraid that— Well, I thought I could escape responsibility by making it seem that he was alive and in good health when I left and . . . well, you know, we parted friends.'

'Did he make passes at you?' Mason asked.

'I tell you, he was unconscious. He was lying on the floor.'

Mason said, 'You're the damnedest little liar I've ever tried to help. For your information, the police are going to be able to *prove* that you were in that cabin for nearly fifteen minutes.'

'I tell you, I wasn't! I didn't— Oh, Mr Mason, won't you *please* believe me? I'm telling you the truth now. I swear to heaven that I am!'

Mason regarded her coldly.

'You're angry with me,' she said. 'You're not going to represent me. You—'

'I've taken your retainer,' Mason said. 'I'm going to represent you. Before I get done I'm going to give you a damn good spanking and see if I can whale the truth out of you.

'Now, Della has told you about the background of this thing, about your father being alive?'

She nodded tearfully.

Mason said, 'You're in a mix-up and—'

The chimes sounded.

Mason frowned thoughtfully for a moment, then said to Della Street, 'See who it is, Della.'

Della Street opened the door.

A uniformed officer said, 'You'll pardon me, but I want to talk with Miss Dianne Alder.'

'What do you want of her?' Mason asked, stepping forward.

'Who are you?' the officer asked.

'I'm Perry Mason. I'm her attorney. I'm representing her on a contract over which there's been a dispute. What do you want of her?'

'We want to question her about a murder.'

'Whose murder?'

'Harrison T. Boring. He was fatally injured earlier this evening. We want to ask Dianne Alder if she knows anything that would help us.'

'Do you folks think she's in any way responsible?' Mason asked.

'We don't know,' the officer said. 'We're trying to piece together what did happen.'

'And why do you want to talk with Dianne Alder?'

'We have a tip.'

'Tips are a dime a dozen,' Mason said.

'The chief sent me to bring her down to headquarters to answer questions.'

'All right,' Mason said, 'she isn't going to headquarters. She's upset and nervous and she's had an emotional shock.'

'In connexion with this case?' the officer asked.

'Don't be silly,' Mason said. 'The emotional shock was in connexion with the loss of a modelling contract which she had expected would lead to movie and television appearances. She's on the verge of hysteria.'

The officer hesitated. 'That may or may not be significant,' he said. 'I was sent to bring her in. I—'

'All right,' Mason said, 'you're not going to bring her in. For the time being she's not going to talk with anyone. She's going to have a strong sedative, and after she gets her emotions under control she'll talk with the chief of police, the prosecuting attorney, or anyone who wants to talk with her. Right now she isn't talking.'

'That's going to put her in rather a peculiar position. It may direct suspicion to her,' the officer said.

'Direct suspicion and be damned!' Mason told him. 'Do you want to adopt the position that the police force of this city is inhuman enough to question an emotionally upset, half-hysterical woman at a time when she's in such an emotional state she should be under the care of a doctor?'

'I'll report to the chief,' the officer said. 'I don't think he'll like it.'

'You do that,' Mason told him, 'and you can tell the chief personally from me, that Dianne Alder is going to be out of circulation until tomorrow morning. She isn't going to answer questions from the newspapers, from the police, or from anyone until she has her nerves under control and has recovered completely from emotional shock.'

'We could take her into custody, you know,' the officer said.

'That's your right,' Mason told him. 'Any time you want to swear out a warrant for her arrest you go right ahead. However, you know and I know that you haven't a scintilla of evidence against her. The only reason that you're here to question her is because you've received an anonymous tip from someone who is trying to add to her troubles. For your information, Officer, this young woman has been the victim of a colossal conspiracy. She's just discovered what has happened and the emotional shock is tremendous.

'If you can assure me that you have one iota of actual evidence against her, we'll try and get a doctor to quiet her nerves and then see if we can get a statement from her. But if you are acting on the strength of an anonymous tip telling you to get hold of her and question her, I'm going to tell you that that anonymous tip comes from the same individuals who have been trying to muscle in on this young woman's property rights – individuals who have played fast and loose with her emotions with absolutely no concern for the outcome.

'Now, what do you want to do?'

The officer grinned and said, 'I guess you called the tune, Mr Mason. In view of that attitude we'll wait until she's in condition to be questioned.'

The officer indicated the tearful, frightened Dianne Alder. 'That is Miss Alder?' he asked.

'That's Miss Alder,' Mason said, 'and the young woman with her is Della Street, my secretary. I'm Perry Mason, her attorney.'

'You'll see she doesn't leave town?' the officer asked.

'I'll be responsible for her,' Mason said.

The officer turned to Dianne. 'I'm sorry, Miss Alder,' he said, and left the room.

Mason said to Della Street, 'Get another suite fast, Della. Get Dianne out of here. Stay in that suite with her tonight. We won't let anyone know where she is. I'll close the door to this bedroom and if anyone who calls on me here jumps to the conclusion that you and she are behind that closed bedroom door, I can't help it.'

Mason turned to Dianne. 'Whatever you do,' he said, 'don't lie. Tell the absolute truth. When you are feeling better you can tell your story in detail to Della Street, but if the police should try to question you, tell them that you aren't going to make any statement except in the presence of your attorney, and send for me. Do you understand?'

Dianne nodded.

'*I* understand,' Della Street said. 'Come on, Dianne, let's go.'

CHAPTER 12

DELLA STREET had been gone less than five minutes when Mason heard a soft code knock on the door; one rap, a pause, four quick raps, a pause, then two raps.

The lawyer made sure the door to the north bedroom of the suite was closed, then crossed the sitting-room, opened the corridor door, and saw Sid Nye on the threshold.

'Hi,' Sid said. 'I just thought I'd pass the word along that the police have a tip on Dianne.'

'I know they do,' Mason said. 'Who gave it to them?'

'Probably Montrose Foster,' Nye said. 'It was an anonymous tip. I also wanted to let you know that you aren't going to have anything to worry about on that time schedule.'

'What do you mean?'

'Moose Dillard had a wrestling match with his conscience and decided that it wasn't necessary for him to make *any* report to the police. Of course, if they question him it's going to be another matter.'

'Did he get out of the place all right?' Mason asked.

'Like a charm,' Nye said.

'What happened?'

'Actually it was pretty simple. I parked my car about a block down the street, walked up to the entrance to the parking place, walked towards the office of the motel as though I were going in there, then detoured around to the side and ducked in at Number 5.'

'No one saw you?'

'I'm quite certain they didn't. They gave no indication if they did.'

'Then what?'

'I scouted the place, then went outside and got in Dillard's car. He'd given me the keys to it. I started the motor, got it warmed up, then gave a signal to Moose. He came out and got in the car and we shot out of there fast.'

'What did you do with the room key?' Mason asked.

'Moose said he left it inside.'

'Then what?'

'I rode around with Moose for a while and talked with him. After that I had him take his car and I got my car. Moose went on his way and I came back here.'

'You say you *talked* with him.'

'That's right.'

'What did you talk with him about?'

'You have two guesses.'

'You didn't make any suggestion that he should duck out, did you?'

'Heavens, no. Far be it from me to make any suggestion like that – perish the thought! Of course, I pointed out to him that if the police wanted to question him they could, but he really didn't have any obligation to do anything except report to Paul Drake – and he's lost his notebook.'

'*Lost* his notebook!' Mason said.

'That's right. It must have dropped from his pocket some-

104

where. Of course I pointed out to him that he'd cut rather a sorry figure if he didn't have that notebook.'

'Look here, Sid, let's be frank. Did you steal that notebook or hide it?'

'Not in that sense of the word. Dillard feels it must have fallen out of his pocket when he was getting in his car. He had his coat over his arm and he tossed the coat into the car.'

'Will the police find it?'

'I don't think so. I saw it when it dropped to the floor of the car. I also have a vague recollection of seeing something fall out when I opened the car door to let Dillard out. I didn't pay much attention to it at the time. I *could* go back and look in the gutter.'

Mason frowned. 'You can't afford to take chances with the police in a murder case, Sid.'

'Sure. I know that. On the other hand, I'm not Dillard's guardian. The guy can go to the police later on if his conscience bothers him.

'Now, what happened in connexion with this anonymous tip on Dianne? Did the police question her?' Nye asked.

'No.'

'Why?'

'I wouldn't let them.'

'The police must be pretty soft here in Riverside.'

'I was pretty hard,' Mason said. 'If they'd had any evidence, they'd have taken her in, but to drag a nice young woman down to headquarters simply on the strength of an anonymous tip is poor business from a public relations standpoint.

'Do you know where Dillard went?'

'I wouldn't have the slightest idea,' Nye said, looking up at the ceiling.

'Suppose we should happen to need him? Suppose we should want to get in touch with him in a hurry?'

'Wherever he is,' Nye said, 'I'm quite certain he reads, or will read, the Riverside papers, and any ad that was put in the classified column would undoubtedly get his attention.'

'I see,' Mason said.

'Well, I must be going,' Nye told him. 'I have quite a few things to do and I wouldn't be too surprised if they didn't put

105

your suite here under surveillance a little later on. It might be just as well if I kept in touch with you by telephone.'

'Your calls will go through a switchboard,' Mason warned.

'Oh, sure,' Nye said. 'I wouldn't say anything that I wouldn't want everybody to hear. Of course if I should talk to you about moose hunting, you'll know what it's all about.'

'Sure,' Mason said, dryly.

'And I can tell you the most likely place we could go to find a moose.'

'I'm quite certain,' Mason said, 'that the information would be of interest to me but only in the event I should want to hunt a moose. Right now I can't imagine anything that would be further from my thoughts.'

Nye grinned, said, 'You know where you can reach me if you want me,' and went out.

For some ten minutes Mason paced the floor thoughtfully, smoking a cigarette, his head bent forward in frowning concentration.

Then the chimes sounded on the door.

Mason crossed over and opened it.

George Winlock stood on the threshold. 'May I come in?' he asked.

'Certainly,' Mason said. 'Come right in, sit down.'

Winlock entered, seated himself, regarded Mason thoughtfully from behind the tinted lenses of his glasses.

Mason said, 'You don't need to wear those now, you know.'

'I've worn them for fourteen years,' Winlock said. 'I really do need them now.'

'You had something in mind?' Mason asked.

Winlock said, 'I have a problem that's bothering me.'

'What is it?'

'Dianne.'

'What about her?'

'I have been pretty much of a heel as far as she is concerned.'

'Do you expect me to argue that point with you?'

'Frankly I do not, but I want to make some sort of settlement, some sort of restitution.'

'Such as what?'

106

'Property.'

'A girl who has been attached to her father and then is led to believe that her father is dead, and subsequently finds out he has been alive all the time but hasn't cared enough about her to lift his finger to get in touch with her, is apt to have lost a good deal of her filial devotion.'

'I can understand that. I thought perhaps you and I could discuss the property end of the situation and then later on, perhaps, Dianne could be made to see things from my viewpoint and realize that under the circumstances there wasn't much else I could have done.'

'I'm afraid that's a viewpoint that will be pretty hard for her to grasp.'

'However,' Winlock said, 'I see no reason for airing all of this in the Press.'

'It will be uncovered.'

'I don't think so.'

'I do,' Mason said. 'Montrose Foster, President of the Missing Heirs and Lost Estates, Inc, is on your trail.'

'Exactly.'

'You knew that?' Mason asked.

'I know it now.'

'You can't hush anything up with Foster nosing around, prying into the background.'

'I'm not entirely certain you're right,' Winlock said. 'Foster is basing his investigation upon the premise Dianne has some relative who died and left an estate in which she could share. Actually there was such a relative, a distant relative of mine, and the estate is small. I feel Foster can be handled in such a way he will go chasing off on a false trail.'

'I see,' Mason said.

'That leaves you,' Winlock said.

'And Dianne,' Mason reminded him.

'Dianne is a very considerate young woman. She isn't going to do anything that would ruin the lives of other people.'

'Meaning the woman who is known as your wife?'

'Yes. I repeat, that leaves you, Mr Mason.'

'It leaves me.'

'I could arrange to see that you received rather a large fee for representing Dianne, perhaps as much as a hundred thousand dollars.'

'I'm representing Dianne,' Mason said. 'I'll do what's best for her.'

'It won't be best for her to make a disclosure of my past and her relationship to me.'

'How do you know it won't?'

'It would simply complicate matters, and get her involved.'

Mason said, 'You're pretty influential here. The police have received an anonymous tip to question Dianne. You should have enough influence to get the police to disregard that anonymous tip. You don't want her questioned – now.'

Winlock thought for a moment, then said, 'Get her out of town.'

'And then?' Mason asked.

'That's all there'll be to it.'

'You can control the police investigation?'

'Within reasonable limits and indirectly, yes.'

'That leaves the question of her property rights,' Mason said.

'Her legal rights to any property are exceedingly nebulous.'

'I don't think so,' Mason said. 'In this state, property acquired after marriage is community property.'

'But I have been separated from my first wife for more than fourteen years.'

'Forget the expression, your first wife,' Mason said. 'You had only one wife.'

'Would that have anything to do with the subject under discussion?'

'A great deal.'

'I'm afraid I fail to follow you, Mr Mason. Eunice Alder is now dead. Property acquired during marriage is community property, but on the death of the wife that property automatically vests in the husband, subject, of course, to certain formalities. If you had approached me prior to the death of Eunice, the situation might have been very different. As matters now stand, I am quite definitely in the saddle.'

'You may think you're in the saddle,' Mason said, 'but you're riding a bucking bronco and you can be thrown for quite a loss. Under the law the wife's interest in the community vests in the husband on her death *unless* she makes a will disposing of her interest in the community property. Your wife made such a will. Dianne is the beneficiary.'

Winlock frowned thoughtfully. 'How much would you want for Dianne?' he asked.

'How much have you got?'

'It depends on how it is evaluated.'

'How do you evaluate it?'

'Perhaps three million, if you consider all of my equities.'

'All right, what's your proposition?'

'I'll liquidate enough holdings to give Dianne five hundred thousand dollars. I will give her fifty thousand dollars within ninety days. I'll pay the balance within a year.'

'And in return for that?'

'In return for that I want absolute, complete silence about our relationship, about my past.'

'All right,' Mason said. 'You're of age. You're supposed to know what you're doing. Now I'll tell you about Dianne. I'm not going to give you any answer. I'm not going to make you any proposition. I'm going to think things over and I'm going to play the cards in the way that will be in the best interests of Dianne Alder.

'If the police find out about her connexion with Harrison T. Boring and question her about her business with Boring, it may well be to Dianne's advantage to disclose the relationship with you, and the whole background.'

'Just so I can have the picture straight,' Winlock said, 'will you summarize briefly Dianne's business with Boring, just what it was?'

Mason said, 'Boring found out about the relationship. He came to Dianne with a lot of legal hocus-pocus pretending he was interested in her as a model who was to appear on television and in movies in connexion with the introduction of a new style in women's garments.

'Back of all that legal hocus-pocus, however, and the bait of television appearances, was the hook that he was to get one half of all of her gross income from any source, inheritance or otherwise. In return for that he was to pay her a hundred dollars a week.

'Last Saturday he sent her notice that the payments would be discontinued. That means he decided it would be better and more profitable, as far as he was concerned, to sink his hooks into you for blackmail rather than to let Dianne collect and then engage in litigation as to whether his contract was any good, whether it had been entered into under false pretences, etc, etc.

'Dianne consulted me about the termination of the contract and the loss of the hundred-dollar-a-week income. She knew nothing about the reason back of the contract.

'I had my suspicions aroused because I was having Harrison Boring shadowed, and so I came to you earlier this evening. Dianne knew nothing about what I was doing. When Montrose Foster found her, and convinced her that in order to protect her good name she must get the other signed copy of the contract back from Boring, she very foolishly failed to consult me but tried to take matters into her own hands.'

'What did she do? Did she call on Boring?'

'I don't think I care to amplify my statement,' Mason said. 'However, the police are following up what apparently was an anonymous telephone tip and want to question her about Boring. They came here and tried to take her to headquarters. I refused to let her go. If they question her, it is quite possible the cat will be out of the bag. I'll do whatever will protect Dianne's best interests.'

'And if they don't question her?' Winlock asked.

'Then,' Mason said, 'I'll take your proposition under advisement and discuss it with Dianne.'

Winlock said, 'Let me use the telephone, if I may.'

He walked over to the telephone, called police headquarters, then after a few moments said, 'Hello, this is George Winlock. I want to talk with Chief Preston. It's quite important that I— Oh, he is? Well, put him on, will you, please?'

There was a moment of silence, then Winlock said, 'Hello, Chief? This is George Winlock. Look here, Chief, you sent someone to question a Dianne Alder at the Mission Inn. What did you want to see her about?'

Winlock was silent for nearly a minute while the telephone made harsh metallic sounds through the receiver.

Then Winlock said, 'That's all it was? Just an anonymous telephone tip? ... All right, Chief, look here. I happen to know something about Dianne Alder. Some people have been attempting to annoy her in connexion with a television modelling contract which she has signed. There are matters of professional jealousy involved, and this anonymous telephone tip, I am satisfied, was inspired by reasons of personal spite and it wouldn't do the slightest good to question her but would embarrass her personally and— Well, thanks a lot, Chief. I thought I'd let you know ... All right, you speak to your men, will you? ... Thanks a lot, goodnight.'

Winlock hung up the telephone. 'Does that answer your question, Mason?'

'That answers my question,' Mason said.

'Get her out of town,' Winlock said.

'Right at the present time,' Mason said, 'she's under sedation.'

'Well, get her out first thing in the morning.'

'Don't you want to see her?'

'She knows all about me?'

'She does now.'

Winlock said, 'Yes, I want to see her, but not here. The situation is too hot. I want her to return to Bolero Beach. I will get in touch with you about a meeting and talk with both you and her about a property settlement.

'In the meantime I trust that I can count on your discretion.'

Mason said, 'You can count on my doing what is best for Dianne's interests.'

Winlock said, 'Please tell her that I called, that she was under sedation, that it was therefore hardly a proper time or a proper place for me to see her. Please tell her that I am using my influence to protect her from any disagreeable publicity, and that I would like to have her reserve judgement about what I have done until she has a chance to hear my side of the story.

'And you might also explain to her,' Winlock went on, 'that

111

I have interceded personally with the police to see that she is not annoyed.'

'That much I can promise you I'll do,' Mason said.

Winlock extended his hand. 'Thank you very much, Mr Mason, and goodnight.'

'Goodnight,' Mason said, and escorted him to the door.

CHAPTER 13

WINLOCK HAD not been gone more than three minutes when Mason heard the chimes and opened the door. A strikingly beautiful woman stood there smiling seductively.

'May I come in, Mr Mason?' she asked. 'I'm Mrs Winlock and I knew my husband was calling on you. I waited behind some potted palms in the lobby until he had left. I want to see you privately.'

'Come in,' Mason invited, 'and sit down.'

'Thanks. I'll come in but I won't sit down. I'll tell you what I want and what I have to offer in a very few words.'

'What do you have to offer?' Mason asked.

'Freedom for Dianne Alder.'

'And what do you want?'

'What I want is to retain my social position, my respectability, and my property interests. Is that clear enough?'

'It's clear enough,' Mason said. 'Now give me the details. What makes you think Dianne Alder's freedom is at stake?'

'Don't be naïve, Mr Mason. Dianne came to Riverside to see Boring. She saw him. She was probably the last person to see him alive.'

'How do you know this?'

'The police have received an anonymous telephone tip to that effect.'

'How do you know that?'

'Through a friend of mine who is in a position to know.'

112

'You seem to know a great deal.'

'Knowledge is power.'

'And you want power?'

'Power and more power. I won't try to deceive you, Mr Mason. There is a concealed microphone in our library. My son is at a romantic age. There have been times when girls have sought to blackmail him. I deemed it wise to have the house wired so conversations could be monitored.'

'And so you heard my conversation with your husband this evening?'

'Every word.'

'All right. Just what is your proposition?'

'If you could prove Harrison Boring was injured – fatally injured – *before* Dianne called on him, it would establish your client's innocence, would it not?'

'Presumably it would,' Mason said.

'I can give you that proof.'

Mason said, 'Perhaps you'd better sit down, Mrs Winlock, and we'll talk this over.'

'Very well.' She moved over to a chair, seated herself, and crossed her knees, adjusting her skirt so that the hemline was where it would be most effective in showing to advantage a pair of very neat nylon-clad legs. She settled back in the chair and smiled at Mason with calm confidence.

'Just how would we go about proving this?' Mason asked.

'That,' she said, 'is a matter of detail which we will discuss later on. The main question is whether you agree with me in principle that if you can establish this matter by definite proof, I am entitled to keep my name, my position, my respectability, and the bulk of my property.'

'What else are you prepared to offer in return?' Mason asked.

'What do you mean by the words, "What else"?'

'What about Dianne's property rights?'

'Does she have any?'

'Yes.'

'What did my husband want?'

'I think perhaps you had better discuss the matter with him.'

'Well, I will put it this way. Whatever proposition my hus-

113

band made in regard to a division of property would be acceptable to me.'

Mason said, 'I'd have to know a little more about how you intend to make this proof and I'd have to discuss it with my client.'

'Very well,' she said. 'Let us suppose that Harrison T. Boring was a blackmailer, a crook, and a promoter. Let us suppose that there were wheels within wheels, that sometime during the evening he became engaged in an altercation with someone who was trying to share in the spoils and, as a result, Boring was fatally injured.

'Now then, let us suppose that my son called on Boring, found him lying injured, but made no specific examination. In fact he assumed that the man was dead drunk, and left. Let us suppose that I called on Boring, found him injured, and came to the conclusion my son had been engaged in an altercation and left the place; that sometime later I phoned the manager of the motel, told her to look in on the man in Unit 10, and hung up.

'Let us assume that my husband followed me in a visit to Boring, found him injured, assumed that I had inflicted the injuries, and left.'

'That would require your testimony, the testimony of your husband, and the testimony of your son, and you would be censured for not calling for aid as soon as you saw the injured man.'

'All of that might be arranged. Tell me, what would be the penalty?'

'If your son thought the man was drunk and had reason so to believe, there would be no violation of the law. If you *knew* that a crime had been committed and failed to report it, the situation might be rather serious.'

'Suppose that I also thought he was drunk?'

'That,' Mason said, 'would present a story which might well tax the credulity of the listener. Two coincidences of that sort would be rather too much.'

'Suppose my husband should admit that he knew the man was injured but thought I had been the one who had struck him with some weapon and that the injury was not serious,

114

that Boring was knocked out. Would the offence be serious enough so that my husband could not be let off with probation and perhaps some admonition and rebuke from the court?'

'Remember,' Mason said, 'that the man died. A great deal would depend on the nature of his injuries, whether a more prompt hospitalization would have resulted in saving his life. Remember also I am Dianne's attorney and am not in a position to advise either you or your husband.'

'Under those circumstances,' she said, 'my proposition had better remain in abeyance.

'I might also mention, Mr Mason, something that you don't seem to have realized – that the room where Mr Boring was found fairly reeked with the smell of whisky.'

Mason raised his eyebrows.

'I gather that you didn't know that.'

'It is always dangerous to jump to conclusions,' Mason said, 'but I am interested in the fact that *you* noticed it.'

She smiled and said, 'You play them rather close to your chest, don't you, Mr Mason?'

'At times I think it is advisable,' Mason said.

Abruptly she arose. 'I have told you generally what I have in mind,' she said, 'and you might think it over. I trust that under the circumstances Dianne will not make any rash statements which would tend to make any meeting of the minds impossible?'

'Are you suggesting,' Mason asked, 'that I suborn perjury?'

'Certainly not, Mr Mason.' She smiled. 'Any more than I am suggesting that I commit perjury. I am simply speculating with you on what would happen under certain circumstances and whether or not it would be possible to bring a situation into existence which would cause those circumstances to be established by evidence.'

'It's an interesting conjecture,' Mason said. 'Now will you tell me exactly what happened when you entered the motel unit rented by Harrison T. Boring?'

'I never even said I was there.'

'I know you were there,' Mason said.

She smiled archly and said, 'Then what you don't know is what I found when I entered the room.'

'Exactly.'

'And under normal circumstances, when would be the first time you would discover this, Mr Mason?'

'When you were placed on the witness stand and examined by the prosecution and I had an opportunity to cross-examine you.'

'And you think you could discover the true facts by cross-examination?'

'I would try.'

'It's an interesting thought,' she said. 'And now, Mr Mason, having given you a brief statement as to the purpose of my visit, I am not going to let you try to trap me by any further conversation.'

She arose, crossed the room with the gracious manner of royalty bestowing a favour, gave Mason her hand, smiled up into his eyes, and said, 'It's been a pleasure meeting you, Mr Mason.'

'I trust we will meet again,' Mason said.

'Oh, I'm sure of it,' she told him. 'My telephone is listed in the book and you can reach me at any time. I will always be available to *your* call.'

Mason watched her down the corridor, then slowly and thoughtfully closed the door.

CHAPTER 14

AT THREE O'CLOCK in the morning Mason was awakened by the persistent ringing of his telephone.

Sleepily, he groped for the instrument, said 'Hello,' and heard Sid Nye's voice.

'Unlock your door. I'm coming up and don't want anyone to see me.'

The connexion was severed before Mason could say a word.

The lawyer rolled out of bed, went to the sitting-room of the suite, and unlocked the door.

A few minutes later Sid Nye slipped into the room.

'You're not going to like this,' he warned.

'Shoot,' Mason said.

'They caught Moose Dillard, evidently nabbed him several hours ago.'

'What do you mean they *caught* him?'

'He was trying to make a getaway and they nabbed him.'

'How come?'

'Well, the police wanted to make a check on persons in adjoining units in the motel to see if any of them had seen or heard anything unusual. They made a door-to-door canvass and everything checked out until they came to the door of Unit 5. Then they found no one home, the door unlocked, the key on the dresser, the bed hadn't been slept in and Dillard had left the curtains slightly parted and the chair in place where he had been sitting looking across at Unit 10 with a whole ashtray full of cigarette stubs on the floor.'

'Keep talking,' Mason said, as Nye hesitated.

'Well, of course, we hadn't figured they'd *search* the other units, but they did. The story was there just as plain as if Dillard had left a written statement of what he'd been doing. There was the chair by the window, the curtains slightly parted, the ashtray full of cigarette stubs giving an indication of how long he'd been watching.'

Mason nodded.

'The police checked on the licence number of Dillard's automobile, found out it was registered to Paul Drake, alerted the California Highway Patrol giving them the licence number of Dillard's automobile and a description of the driver. They also alerted the city police with a radio bulletin. As it happened, one of the city police picked up Dillard at a service station on the outskirts of town where he was gassing up.'

'Then what happened?'

'Well, they checked on Dillard's driving licence, his occupation, found he was a private detective, started asking him why he was so anxious to get out of town, and intimated that he might have a little more licence trouble if he didn't cooperate.

117

'That was all Dillard needed. He'd been through the mill once and he didn't want any more beefs.'

'So he spilled everything he knew?'

'Everything. He even took them to the place where we'd "lost" the notebook. It was still there lying by the kerb. They nailed it. Of course, that showed Dianne was the last one to see Boring alive, or presumably alive; that she had dashed out of the place, her manner showing great excitement and emotional disturbance.

'The bad thing is that Dillard insists Dianne was in the room almost fifteen minutes. The police didn't like that.'

'And *I* don't like it,' Mason said. 'She swears she wasn't.'

'Time could pass pretty fast if she was looking for something,' Nye said.

'Not that fast,' Mason said, frowning. 'There's no chance Moose Dillard could have been mistaken?'

'Hell, no. Not on a deal like that. Moose is a little slow thinking sometimes. He's quick-tempered and he makes mistakes, but as an operative he's tops. He knows what he's doing, he keeps notes, he's a good observer and you can depend on his data.'

Mason was thoughtfully silent.

'It's a hell of a mess,' Sid Nye said.

'It's tough,' Mason admitted, 'but we're going to have to face conditions as they are and not the way we'd like to have them. You can't argue with a fact.

'Why haven't they arrested Dianne, Sid?'

'I don't know. Perhaps they're waiting for—'

The telephone rang

Mason answered it.

Della Street said, 'There's a policewoman here in the room and she has a warrant for Dianne.'

'Let Dianne go with her,' Mason said. 'And tell Dianne not to make *any* statement except in my presence. Tell her to say *nothing – nothing.*'

'I'll tell her,' Della Street said.

'Stall along as much as you can, Della. I'll be down as soon as I can get some clothes on.'

'Will do,' she promised.

118

Mason started dressing, talking to Sid Nye as he hurried into his clothes.

'Sid, I want you to get out of town while the getting's good. You're not a witness to anything and therefore it won't be concealing evidence to have you hard to find. However, right at the moment I don't want the police inquiring into *my* activities after I came to Riverside.'

'You don't want anyone to know you called on Winlock?'

Mason buttoned his shirt. 'That's right, and I don't care about having the police know Winlock called on Boring ... Will Dillard be able to tell them it was Winlock, his wife, and stepson who called on Boring?'

'No. He doesn't have their licence numbers or names. He has the general descriptions of two of the automobiles and descriptions of the people. The only licence number he has is that on Dianne's car. He can, of course, make an identification if they confront him with the persons but there's nothing that would lead them to the Winlocks from his description; in fact, the Winlocks would be the last persons they'd suspect in a case of this sort.'

Mason fastened his belt. 'And remember, in case you're questioned, *you* don't *know* who Boring's callers were. You've only surmised – and the same is true of me.'

Mason hurried down to Della Street's room and a police-woman answered his knock.

'Good morning,' Mason said. 'I'm Perry Mason. I'm Dianne Alder's attorney. Do I understand you're taking her into custody?'

'Yes.'

'I want to talk with her.'

'She isn't dressed. I'm taking her into custody. You'll have to talk with her at headquarters.'

Mason raised his voice. 'I'll talk to her through the door. Say absolutely nothing, Dianne. Don't tell the police about your name, your past, your parents, or—'

The door slammed in the lawyer's face.

Mason waited some ten minutes in the corridor until the policewoman, accompanied by Della Street and Dianne Alder, emerged into the corridor.

'Can you take it, Dianne?' Mason asked. 'Can you keep quiet?'

Dianne nodded.

The policewoman turned on him. 'I don't want lawyers addressing my prisoner,' she said. 'If you want to consult with your client, you can come to the jail and do it in a regular manner.'

'What's wrong with this?' Mason asked.

'It's against my orders. If you persist I'll have to charge you with interfering with an arrest.'

'Is it a crime,' Mason asked, 'to advise a client in the presence of an arresting officer, that if she once starts answering any questions the point at which she stops will be considered significant, but if she doesn't answer any questions at all on the advice of her counsel, and demands an immediate hearing, she is—'

'That will do,' the policewoman said angrily. 'You're talking to her.'

'I'm talking to you.'

'Well, your words are aimed at her. I'm going to ask you and Miss Street to leave now. That's an order.'

Mason smiled. 'My, but you're hard to get along with.'

'I can be,' she said angrily.

Dianne Alder dropped a pace behind so that she was looking over the officer's shoulder at Perry Mason. She raised her forefinger to her lips in a gesture of silence.

Mason bowed to the officer. 'I accede to your wishes, madam. Come on, Della.'

CHAPTER 15

CARTER LELAND, the district attorney of Riverside County, said to the magistrate, 'If the Court please, this is a simple matter of a preliminary hearing. We propose to show that the defendant in this case had a business arrangement with the decedent, Harrison T. Boring; that she became convinced Boring had swindled her, that she was exceedingly indignant, that she went to the Restawhile Motel in order to see him and did see him; that she was the last person to see Boring alive and that when she left the room Boring was in a dying condition.

'That is all we need to show, in fact more than we need to show, in order to get an order binding the defendant over for trial.'

'Put on your case,' Judge Warren Talent said.

'My first witness is Montrose Foster,' Leland announced.

Montrose Foster came forward, held up his right hand, was sworn, seated himself nervously on the witness stand.

'Your name is Montrose Foster, you reside in Riverside and have for some two years last past? You are the president of Missing Heirs and Lost Estates?'

'That is true.'

'On last Tuesday, the day of the murder as charged in the complaint, did you have occasion to talk with the defendant?'

'I did.'

'Where did this conversation take place?'

'At Bolero Beach.'

'Did the defendant make any statement to you about her feeling towards Harrison T. Boring?'

'She did.'

'What did she say?'

'She said she could kill him.'

Leland turned abruptly and unexpectedly to Perry Mason. 'Cross-examine,' he said.

'Is that all you're going to bring out on direct examination?' Mason asked.

'It's enough,' Leland snapped. 'I don't intend to let this preliminary hearing become a three-ring circus.'

Mason turned to the witness. 'Did you,' he asked, 'say something to the defendant that was well calculated to cause her to make that statement?'

'Objected to,' Leland said, 'as calling for a conclusion of the witness. He can't testify as to what was in the defendant's

121

mind or what was calculated to arouse certain emotions, but only to facts.'

'Sustained,' Judge Talent said. 'I think you can reframe the question, Mr Mason.'

'I'll be glad to, Your Honour,' Mason said, and turned to the witness. 'Did you *try* to say something that would be calculated to arouse her rage towards the decedent?'

'Why, Your Honour,' Leland said, 'that's exactly the same question. That's a repetition of the same question calling for a conclusion of the witness and in defiance of the ruling of the Court.'

'No, it isn't,' Mason said. 'This question now relates to the state of mind of the witness.'

'And that's completely immaterial,' Leland said.

Mason grinned. 'You mean I can't show his bias?'

Leland started to say something, caught himself.

Judge Talent smiled and said, 'The question has been skilfully reframed. The objection is overruled.'

'I told her certain things about Boring,' Foster said.

'The question, Mr Foster, was whether you tried to arouse her anger against Boring by what you told her.'

'Very well. The answer is yes.'

'You deliberately tried to arouse the defendant's anger?'

'I told you, yes.'

'Did you tell her that Boring had been attempting to sell her into white slavery?'

'Well – that was her idea.'

'You agreed with it?'

'I didn't disagree with it.'

'At no time during the conversation did you mention that Boring's purpose in his dealings with her was one of immorality?'

'Well, she brought that subject up herself.'

'And you, in your conversation, encouraged her in that belief?'

'Yes.'

'And told her that Boring had deceived her in order to get her to sign an agreement which was intended to enable him to sell her into white slavery?'

'I didn't tell her that. She told me that.'

'You agreed with her?'

'Yes.'

'And then, after that, you told her that *was* Boring's objective?'

'All right, I did.'

Mason smiled. 'Now, *you* knew what Boring was after, didn't you, Mr Foster? Didn't you tell me that Boring had located some property and an estate to which the defendant could establish title?'

'That's what he was after, yes.'

'And you knew what he was after?'

'Of course I did.'

'Then that was his real objective?'

'Yes.'

'Therefore when you told the defendant that the purpose of Boring's contract with her was to get her in his power for other reasons, you lied to her?'

'I let her deceive herself.'

'Answer the question,' Mason said. 'When you told her that, you lied to her?'

'That's objected to – it's not proper cross-examination,' Leland said. 'It also assumes facts not in evidence.'

'Objection overruled on both counts,' Judge Talent said.

'All right,' Foster snapped, 'I lied to her.'

'You did that in order to get an advantage for yourself?'

'Yes.'

'You are, then, willing to lie as a part of your everyday business transactions in order to get an advantage for yourself?'

'I didn't say that,' the witness said.

'I'm asking it,' Mason said.

'The answer is no.'

'You don't generally lie in order to get an advantage for yourself?'

'That certainly is objectionable, Your Honour,' Leland said.

'I think so. The objection is sustained,' Judge Talent ruled.

'But you did tell such a lie in order to get such an advantage in *this* case?' Mason asked.

123

'Yes,' the witness snapped.

'Now, on the evening of the murder, you yourself saw Harrison T. Boring at the Restawhile Motel, did you not?'

'Yes.'

'And had an interview with the decedent?'

'Yes.'

'Your Honour,' Leland said, 'the prosecution wishes to object to any testimony as to what took place at that interview. It was not brought out on direct examination, and if counsel wants to go into it, he must make this witness his own witness.'

'I think it shows motivation and bias,' Mason said.

'I'm inclined to agree with you,' Judge Talent said. 'I think you can at least show the bias and interest of this witness, and if it appears that he himself was in contact with the decedent on the day of the murder, that may well establish an interest.'

Mason turned to the witness. 'Did you lie to Boring at the time you had that interview with him ?'

'No.'

'You didn't tell him that this defendant was going to re-pudiate any arrangement she might have with him, but that if Boring would let you in on the secret of what he had dis-covered, you would cooperate with Boring and would keep the defendant in line and you would share whatever property she was entitled to fifty-fifty – words to that effect?'

'That was generally the nature of my proposition.'

'But you didn't have the defendant tied up with any agree-ment?'

'I felt I could secure such an agreement.'

'But you told Boring you had her tied up?'

'Something of that sort.'

'So you lied to Boring?'

'All right!' the witness shouted. 'I lied to Boring. He lied to me and I lied to him.'

'Whenever it suits your advantage, you're willing to lie?' Mason asked.

'If the Court please,' Leland said, 'that's the same question that has already been ruled on. I object to it.'

'Sustained,' Judge Talent said.

'So, on last Tuesday,' Mason said, 'in connexion with your

ordinary business activities, in two interviews you told lies in order to get an advantage for yourself.'

'Same objection,' Leland said. 'It's the same question, Your Honour.'

'I don't think it is,' Judge Talent said. 'It is now a specific question as to two interviews with two people. However, I'm going to sustain the objection on the ground that the question has already been asked and answered. The witness had admitted lying to each of two people on the same day.'

Mason turned to the witness. 'And are you lying now?'

'No.'

'Would you lie if it suited your advantage?'

'Objected to as not proper cross-examination, and as argumentative,' Leland said.

'Sustained,' Judge Talent said.

'Did you have any physical altercation with Boring at the time you saw him?'

'I— It depends on what you mean by a physical altercation.'

'Did Boring hit you?'

'No.'

'Did he grab you by the coat or other garment?'

'He pushed me.'

'Did he throw you out?'

'He tried to.'

'But wasn't man enough to do it?'

'No.'

'Because you resisted him?'

'Yes.'

'And how did you resist him?'

'I poked him one.'

'So,' Mason said, smiling, 'on the day of Boring's death, on this Tuesday evening, you went to see the decedent shortly before his death. You had lied to the defendant, you lied to Boring, you engaged in a struggle with him and you poked him. Is that right?'

'All right, that's right,' Foster said.

'You had reason to believe Boring had a large sum of money on him and you demanded that he surrender a part or all of that money to you – that he divide it with you?'

'Objected to as not proper cross-examination,' Leland said.

Judge Talent thought the matter over, then said, 'I'm going to sustain that objection.'

'*Did* you get some money from him?' Mason asked.

'Same objection.'

'Same ruling.'

'No further questions,' Mason said.

'That's all,' Leland said. 'I'll call Steven Dillard as my next witness.'

Moose Dillard lumbered to the stand, his huge frame seeming to sag inside of his coat. His eyes were downcast and he studiously avoided Perry Mason.

'What's your name?' Leland asked.

'Steven Dillard.'

'What's your occupation?'

'I'm a detective.'

'A private detective?'

'Yes, sir.'

'Were you employed as such on last Tuesday?'

'Yes.'

'Did you know the decedent, Harrison T. Boring?'

'I had seen him.'

'When had you first seen him?'

'On Monday.'

'Where?'

'Leaving Perry Mason's office.'

'And what did you do with reference to following him?'

'I had put an electronic bug on his automobile.'

'By that you mean an electronic device for the purpose of enabling you to follow the automobile?'

'Yes.'

'Can you describe this device?'

'It is a battery-powered device which was attached to his car and which sends out signals which are received by a companion device attached to the car I was driving. By using it I didn't need to get close to the car I was tailing.'

'And you thereafter shadowed Mr Boring?'

'Yes.'

126

'You followed him to the Restawhile Motel in Riverside?'

'Yes.'

'And as a part of your shadowing operations secured a unit directly across from him?'

'That's right.'

'What time did you check into that unit on last Tuesday?'

'At about six o'clock in the evening.'

'Did you keep Unit 10, in which Harrison Boring was registered, under surveillance?'

'I did.'

'During that evening did you see the defendant?'

'I did.'

'At what time?'

'I kept some notes. May I look at those notes?'

'Those notes were made by you?'

'Yes.'

'They are in your handwriting?'

'Yes.'

'And were made at the time?'

'Yes.'

The district attorney nodded. 'You may consult the notes for the purpose of refreshing your recollection.'

Dillard said, 'The defendant came to his cabin at about nine o'clock and left at nine-twelve.'

'Are you certain of your time, Mr Dillard?'

'Absolutely.'

'Do you know that your watch was correct?'

'It is my custom to carry an accurate watch, and when I am on a job I make it my habit to check the watch with the radio.'

'Did you notice anything about the defendant's manner that would indicate emotional agitation when she left?'

'She was in a tremendous hurry. She almost ran out of the unit and around to the side of her automobile and jumped in the car.'

'You recognized the defendant?'

'Yes.'

'You took down the licence number of the automobile she was driving?'

'Yes.'

'What was it?'

'It was TNM 148.'

'Did you subsequently check the registration slip on that automobile?'

'I did.'

'And what name appears on that registration slip fastened to the steering wheel of the automobile?'

'The name of Dianne Alder.'

'And after she left, who else went into the Boring cabin?'

'No one, until the manager of the motel looked in just long enough to open the door, step inside, then hurry out.'

'And after that, who else came?'

'Two police officers.'

'And after that, who else went in?'

'Two stretcher bearers.'

'This was while the police were there?'

'Yes.'

'Then, from the time the defendant left that cabin, no one else entered the cabin until the officers came. Is that right?'

'That's right.'

'Cross-examine,' Leland snapped to Perry Mason.

'I may have misunderstood your testimony,' Mason said. 'I thought you said that from the time the defendant left the cabin no one entered it until the officers entered.'

'That's right.'

'How about the manager of the hotel? Didn't she enter?'

'Well, she just looked in and out.'

'What do you mean by *looked* in?'

'Opened the door and looked in.'

'Did she enter the unit?'

'It depends on what you mean by enter. She stood there in the doorway.'

'Did she step inside?'

'Yes.'

'Did she close the door behind her?'

'I . . . I don't think so.'

'You have your notebook there in which you kept track of the times?'

'Yes.'

'May I see that notebook?' Mason asked.

The witness handed it over.

Mason said, 'You show that a man who was driving a sports car entered the unit.'

'That was earlier.'

'Then another man entered the unit, a man who, according to your notes, wore dark glasses.'

'Your Honour,' Leland said, 'if the Court please, I object to this line of interrogation. The purpose of my examination was to show only that the defendant entered the building and was the last person to see the decedent alive; that she was in there a full twelve minutes and that when she departed she was greatly agitated.

'Now then, the witness has refreshed his memory from notes made at the time. Mr Mason is entitled to examine him on those notes only for the purpose of showing the authenticity of the notes. He cannot go beyond the scope of legitimate cross-examination and ask questions about matters which were not covered in my direct examination.'

'I think under the circumstances that places an undue restriction upon the cross-examination,' Judge Talent said.

Leland remained standing. 'If the Court please, I don't want to argue with Your Honour, but this is a very vital matter. It is possible to confuse the issues if the door is open on cross-examination to a lot of collateral matters. This is only a preliminary hearing. I only need to show that a crime was committed and that there is reasonable ground to connect the defendant with the commission of that crime. That is the only purpose of this hearing and that's all I need to show.'

Judge Talent turned to Mason. 'Would you like to be heard on this, Counsellor?'

'I would,' Mason said. 'It is my contention that the testimony of this witness is valueless without his notes. I propose to show that his notes are inaccurate and then I am going to move to strike out his entire evidence.'

'You aren't trying at this time, by cross-examining him about other persons who entered the unit, to do anything other than question the validity of his notes?'

'That is the primary purpose of my examination.'

'Objection overruled,' Judge Talent said. 'You may certainly examine him on his notes.'

'Answer the question,' Mason said.

'My notes show that a man entered at eight and was out at eight-fifteen; that another man entered at eight-twenty and was out at eight thirty-five; that a woman entered at eight thirty-six and was out at eight forty-five; that a man in dark glasses entered at eight forty-six and was out at eight-fifty; that the defendant entered at nine and was out at nine-twelve.'

'When was the last time you saw the decedent?' Mason asked.

'When he entered Unit 10.'

'You didn't see him personally come to the door to admit any of these people whom you have mentioned in your notes?'

'No ... Now, wait a minute. I did see the decedent go out to the parking lot where my car was parked and look at the registration. That was shortly after we had checked in at the motel, sometime before he had any visitors.'

'I'm not asking about that at this time,' Mason said, 'I notice that your notes show nothing after nine-twelve.'

'That's when the defendant went out.'

'And your notes show nothing else?'

'That was when I quit taking notes.'

'Why did you quit taking notes? Did you know the man was dead?' Mason asked.

'Oh, Your Honour, I object to that,' Leland said. 'That question is absurd.'

'There must have been some reason the man stopped taking notes,' Judge Talent said. 'I think counsel is entitled to cross-examine him about his notes. The objection is overruled.'

'Well, I quit taking notes when the defendant left because ...'

'Because what?' Mason asked.

'Because you and my boss were there personally and you could see for yourself what went on.'

'Oh, I see,' Mason said. 'Then you quit taking notes when I came to the cabin. Is that right?'

'Yes.'

'And you want us to understand that your notes are accurate up to that time?'

'Yes.'

'But,' Mason said, 'your notes don't show the arrival of the police officers. Your notes don't show the arrival of the ambulance.'

'Well, I told you about them.'

'But you didn't know we were going to come.'

'I expected you.'

'So you quit taking notes when you expected we would come.'

'Well, I didn't think it was necessary to take notes on those. That wasn't why I was shadowing the man.'

'And,' Mason said, 'your notes don't show the time the manager of the motel entered that unit, how long she was in there, or when she came out.'

'Well, she just looked in and out and I didn't think that was important.'

'Oh,' Mason said, 'you want us then to understand that your notes only show the matters that you considered important. In other words, if anyone entered the unit and you didn't think that person was important, it doesn't show in your notes.'

'Well, I— All right,' Dillard blurted, 'I overlooked a bit there. I didn't put down the time the manager came in.'

'Or the time she went out?'

'She came in and went out all at the same time.'

'Came and went in the same instant?' Mason asked, feigning incredulity.

'Well, you know what I mean. She went in and – she was only in there a second and then she came running out.'

'There was a telephone in the unit which you occupied?'

'Yes.'

'And you mentioned that you had a boss there in Riverside?'

'A man who was above me in the organization for which I am working, yes.'

'You are referring to Sidney Nye?'

'Yes.'

'And you called Sidney Nye?'

131

'Yes.'

'When?'

'Right after the manager of the motel came running out. I figured there was something wrong.'

'Let's see if I can understand the floor plan of the room which you occupied. There was a bed in that room?'

'Yes.'

'A chair?'

'Yes.'

'There was a window looking out on the parking place, and by sitting at that window you could look across and see the entrance to Unit 10?'

'Yes.'

'And there was a telephone?'

'Yes.'

'Where was the telephone?'

'By the bed.'

'Now, after you saw the manager come running out, you went to the telephone and called a report in to Sid Nye, didn't you?'

'Well, I didn't report but I gave him the signal something was wrong.'

'And what did you say?'

'I got him on the phone and said, "Hey Rube".'

'You had previously worked in a circus?'

'Yes.'

'And "Hey Rube" is a rallying cry for the circus people to unite in a fight against the outsiders?'

'Something to that effect, yes.'

'Did you have any trouble in getting Sid Nye?'

'No, he answered the phone as soon as it rang.'

'I asked you,' Mason said, 'if you had any trouble in getting Sid Nye.'

'Well, yes. The manager, of course, was busy notifying the police and—'

'You don't know what the manager was doing,' Mason said. 'You couldn't see her, could you?'

'No.'

'Then you don't know *what* she was doing.'

132

'Well, I surmised what she was doing because I had to sit at the phone for such a long time before anyone answered.'

'You knew that the calls went through a switchboard there in the office?'

'Yes.'

'And she had to connect you with an outside line?'

'I had to give her the number and she would call it.'

'Now, while you were at the phone, you had your back to the window, didn't you?'

'I couldn't be in two places at the same time.'

'Exactly,' Mason said. 'You had previously called Sid Nye, earlier in the evening, hadn't you?'

'No, I— Yes, wait a minute, I did. I told him I had been made.'

'What did you mean by that?'

'I meant that the subject had become suspicious and gone out and had looked at the registration certificate on my car.'

'That was the last time you saw him?'

'Yes.'

'And while he was doing that you telephoned Sid Nye?'

'No, I waited until after he'd turned his back and gone into the motel unit that he occupied.'

'That was Unit Number 10?'

'Yes.'

'And then you telephoned Sid Nye and told him you had been made?'

'Yes.'

'Any other conversation?'

'That was about it.'

'Didn't you tell him you were hungry?'

'Well, that's right. I asked him if I should go out to dinner.'

'And what did he say?'

'No. He told me to sit tight. He – I think he was in your room at the time and was talking with you and relaying your instructions.'

'And during that time you were at the telephone?'

'Of course I was at the phone.'

'And had your back turned towards the window?'

'Yes.'

133

'So,' Mason said, 'as far as your notes are concerned they are inaccurate and incomplete in that they don't show anything that happened after the defendant left the unit.'

'There wasn't anything else that happened, except that the police came.'

'And the manager of the motel?'

'And the manager of the motel.'

'And, during the time you had your back turned while you were telephoning or trying to get a connexion through the switchboard, any number of people could have come and gone.'

'Well – like I told you, Mr Mason, I couldn't be in two places at the same time.'

'So,' Mason said, 'as far as you know, Boring wasn't in Unit 10 at all during the time the defendant was there.'

'How do you mean?'

'The decedent could have left that unit while you were telephoning Nye to tell him that you had been made, as you expressed it, and the decedent could have again entered the unit after the manager had entered the unit and then left in a hurry, and while you were telephoning Sid Nye to say *Hey Rube*.'

'All right,' Dillard said, 'I kept the place under surveillance but I can't be everyplace at once. Naturally when I was at the telephone I couldn't be there at the window, and when I went to the bathroom I wasn't there.'

'Oh,' Mason said, 'then you weren't at the window *all* of the time.'

'No. I did a reasonable job of surveillance and that's all you can expect.'

'So your notes are inaccurate in that they don't show *every* person who came to the unit and they don't show every person who left.'

'Those notes are accurate.'

'They show the persons that you saw entering and the persons you saw leaving,' Mason said, 'but you don't know how many other people could have gone in or gone out that you didn't see.'

'I'd have seen them, all right.'

'But you were in the bathroom on at least one occasion?'

134

'Yes.'

'Perhaps two?'

'Perhaps.'

'And you didn't put down the time the manager of the motel was in there?'

'No.'

'Or the time she left?'

'No.'

'That's all,' Mason said.

'If the Court please,' Leland said, 'I intended to let that conclude my case but under the circumstances and in view of the highly technical point raised by counsel I will call the manager of the motel.

'Mrs Carmen Brady, will you come forward and be sworn, please?'

Mrs Brady was sworn, identified herself as the manager of the motel.

'On Tuesday night did you have occasion to go to Unit 10?'

'I did.'

'What time was this?'

'I made a note of the time. It was exactly nine-twelve.'

'And what happened?'

'The telephone rang and a woman's voice said that I had better check on the man in Unit 10, that he seemed to be ill. I hung up the telephone, went to the unit, and looked in and Mr Boring was lying there on the floor. He was breathing laboriously and heavily and I dashed back and called the police.'

'Cross-examine,' Leland snapped at Perry Mason.

'What time did this call come in?' Mason asked.

'At twelve minutes past nine.'

'You went to the unit?'

'Yes.'

'How long were you in there?'

'No time at all. I opened the door and saw this man lying on the floor and turned and dashed out and notified the police.'

'At once?'

'At once.'

'Did you close the door behind you when you entered the motel unit?'

'I . . . I can't remember, Mr Mason. I think I started to close the door and then saw the man on the floor and was startled and ran towards him. I bent over him and saw he was still alive and then I dashed out of the unit and called the police.'

'How do you fix the time of the call as being nine-twelve?'

'I made a note of it.'

'At the suggestion of the police?'

'Yes.'

'Then you marked down the time, *not at the time the phone call was received but at some time afterwards*?'

'Within a few minutes afterwards.'

'How long afterwards?'

'Well, I called the police and told them the man was injured, and they wanted to know how I knew and I told them about having received a tip over the telephone, and the police officer suggested that I make a note of the time.'

'So you made a note of the time.'

'Yes.'

'And what time was that?'

'It was just a little after nine-thirteen.'

'Then you made a note of nine-twelve, a little after nine-thirteen?'

'Well, I thought the call had been received a minute earlier.'

Mason said, 'You received this call. You hung up the telephone and went at once to Unit 10?'

'Yes.'

'And then went back to the motel and then picked up the telephone and called the police.'

'Yes.'

'How far is it from the office to the motel unit?'

'Not over seventy-five feet.'

'Did the police tell you it was then nine-thirteen?'

'Not at the time, no.'

'How did you fix the time?'

'By the electric clock in the office.'

'And did that clock show the time as nine-thirteen?'

The witness hesitated.

'Did it?' Mason asked. 'Yes or no?'

'No. The clock showed the time as nine-seventeen.'

'Yet you now swear it was actually nine-thirteen?'

'Yes.'

'On what basis?'

'The police records show I called at nine-thirteen. Their time is accurate to the second. Later on when I checked my clock I found it was fast.'

'When did you check it?'

'The next day.'

'You did that after you found there was a discrepancy between your time and that on the police records?'

'Yes.'

'I think that's all,' Mason said. 'I have no further questions.'

'I'll call Dr Powers to the stand,' Leland said.

Dr Powers took the stand.

'Did you have occasion to perform an autopsy on a body on Wednesday morning?'

'I did.'

'Had you previously seen that individual?'

'I had treated him when he arrived in an ambulance at the emergency room.'

'What was his condition at that time?'

'He was dying.'

'When did he die?'

'About twenty minutes after his arrival.'

'Do you know the cause of death?'

'A fracture of the skull. He had been hit with some blunt instrument on the back of the head.'

'He was hit with a blunt instrument, Doctor?'

'As nearly as I can tell.'

'There was a fracture of the skull?'

'Yes.'

'And it resulted in death?'

'Yes.'

'Cross-examine,' Leland said.

'There was no external haemorrhage?' Perry Mason asked.

'No.'

'An internal haemorrhage?'

'Yes. Within the skull there was a massive haemorrhage.'

'Injuries of this sort could have been sustained by a fall, Doctor?'

'I don't think so. The portion of the skull in question had received a very heavy blow from some heavy object.'

'Such as a club?'

'Perhaps.'

'A hammer?'

'I would say, more in the nature of a bar of some sort.'

'Perhaps a pipe.'

'Perhaps.'

'Did you notice any other injuries?'

'Well, I noticed a contusion on the side of the man's face, a rather slight contusion but nevertheless a contusion.'

'You mean a bruise?'

'Yes.'

'Technically a traumatic ecchymosis?'

'Yes.'

'Any other injuries?'

'No.'

'No further questions,' Mason said.

'I'll call Herbert Knox,' Leland said.

Knox came forward, was sworn, identified himself as an officer, stated that he had received a radio report at nine-fifteen to go to the Restawhile Motel; that he arrived at approximately nine-eighteen, was directed to Unit 10; that he there found a man who was injured, that this was the same man who had been taken to the emergency unit and turned over to Dr Powers, the witness who had just testified; that the man was then, in his opinion, in a dying condition and that the witness subsequently saw the body in the morgue and it was the body of the same individual he had first seen in Unit 10 at the Restawhile Motel.

'Cross-examine,' Leland said.

'Did you notice the odour of whisky in the unit?' Mason asked.

'I certainly did. Whisky had been spilled over the clothes of the injured man. The odour was strong.'

'You made an inventory of the things in the room?'

'Later on, yes.'

'There was a travelling bag and some clothes?'

'Yes, a two-suiter and a travelling bag.'

'Did you find any money?'

'Not in the unit, no.'

'Did you at any time search the injured man for money?'

'Not until after his arrival at the hospital. I personally searched the clothes which were removed from him.'

'Did you find any money?'

'A hundred and fifteen dollars and twenty-two cents in bills and coins,' the officer said.

'There was no more?'

'No. He was wearing a money belt. It was empty.'

'Did you search Boring's automobile?'

'Yes.'

'Did you find any money?'

'No.'

'As far as you know, the money which you have mentioned represented the entire cash which he had?'

'Yes.'

'That's all,' Mason said.

'That's our case, if the Court please,' Leland said. 'We ask that the defendant be bound over for trial.'

'Does the defence wish to make any showing?' Judge Talent asked. 'If not, it would seem that the order should be made. This is simply a preliminary hearing and it has been established that a crime has been committed and that there is at least reasonable ground to believe the defendant is connected with the commission of the crime.'

Mason said, 'It is now eleven-thirty. May I ask the Court for a recess until two o'clock, at which time the defence will decide whether we wish to put on any case?'

'Very well,' Judge Talent said. 'We'll continue the case until two PM. Will that give you sufficient time, Mr Mason?'

'I think so, yes,' Mason said.

After court adjourned, newspaper reporters interviewed Mason and Leland briefly.

Leland, coldly aloof, said, 'I am fully familiar with counsel's reputation for turning a preliminary hearing into a major courtroom controversy. It is entirely improper and, if I

139

may say so without criticizing my brother district attorneys, I think the reason is that some of those district attorneys have become a little gun shy of Mr Mason. They try to put too much evidence and that gives the defence an opportunity to make a grandstand showing.'

The newspaper reporter turned to Mason. 'Any comment?' he asked.

Mason grinned and said, 'I'll make my comment at two o'clock this afternoon,' and walked out.

CHAPTER 16

MASON, DELLA STREET, and Paul Drake ordered lunch to be served in their suite at the Mission Inn.

The telephone rang shortly after Mason had placed the order.

Della Street nodded to Mason. 'For you, Chief,' she said, and then added in a low voice, 'Mrs W.'

Mason took the phone, said, 'Hello,' and Mrs Winlock's smooth, cool voice came floating over the line.

'Good afternoon, Mr Mason. How did the court hearing go this morning?'

'Very much as I expected,' Mason said cautiously.

'And do you want to do something that is for the best interests of your client?'

'Very much.'

'If,' the voice said, 'you will adhere to the bargain I outlined to you, you should be able to score another triumph over the prosecution, have the defendant released, and have the case thrown out of court.

'Both my son and I are in a position to testify, if necessary, that when we entered that unit the man was lying on the floor breathing heavily and we thought he was drunk. And I will

140

testify that I was the one who made the phone call to the manager of the motel.'

'Suppose I simply subpoena you and put you on the stand?' Mason asked.

She laughed and said, 'Come, come, Mr Mason, you're a veteran attorney. You could hardly commit a booboo of that sort. Think of what it would mean if I should state the man was alive and well when I left.'

'And your price?' Mason asked.

'You know my price. Complete, utter silence about matters which will affect my property status and my social status. Goodbye, Mr Mason.'

The receiver clicked at the other end of the line.

Della Street raised inquiring eyebrows.

Mason said, 'Paul, you're going to have to pick up lunch somewhere along the line. I want you to go out to the Rest-awhile Motel. I want you to take a stop watch. I want you to get the manager to walk rapidly from the switchboard, out the front door, down to Unit 10. I want you to have her open the door, walk inside, turn around, walk back, pick up the telephone, call police headquarters, and ask what time it is. See how long it takes and report to me.'

'Okay,' Drake said. 'What time do you want me back here?'

'Call in,' Mason said. 'I may have something else for you. Telephone a report just as soon as you have checked the time.'

'Okay,' Drake said, 'on my way.'

Five minutes after Drake had left, the chimes in the suite sounded, and Della Street opened the door to a very agitated George D. Winlock.

'Good afternoon,' Winlock said. 'May I come in?'

'Certainly. Come right in,' Mason said.

Winlock looked at Della Street. 'I would like very much to have a completely private conversation with you, Mr Mason.'

'You can't do it,' the lawyer said. 'Under the circumstances I'm not going to have any conversation with you without a witness. However, I may state that Miss Street is my con-fidential secretary and has been such for quite some time. You can trust to her discretion, but she'll listen to what's said and, what's more, she'll take notes.'

Winlock said, 'This is a very, very delicate matter, Mr Mason. It is very personal.'

'She's heard delicate matters before which have been very, very personal,' Mason said.

Winlock debated the matter for a moment, then surrendered. 'You leave me no choice, Mr Mason.'

'Sit down,' Mason said. 'Tell me what's on your mind.'

Winlock said, 'My wife has told you that she and her son, Marvin Harvey Palmer, are willing to testify that they were the two people who were seen entering Unit 10 between eight and nine; that at that time Boring was lying on the floor breathing heavily; that they smelled whisky and thought he was lying there drunk; that Marvin Palmer waited for some minutes, hoping that Boring would revive so that he could talk with him; that my wife was there a much shorter period of time.'

'Well?' Mason asked.

'It's not true,' Winlock said, with some agitation. 'Boring was in full possession of his health and his faculties when they were there.'

'How do you know?'

'Because I was there after they were.'

'You haven't told me,' Mason said, 'what was the nature of your interview with Boring.'

'I told him I was going to have him arrested for blackmail, that there was no longer any opportunity to keep my relationship with Dianne secret, that you had uncovered it and that Dianne herself knew about it, that under the circumstances I was going to have him arrested in the event he wasn't out of town by morning.'

'Did you ask him for the ten thousand dollars back?'

'Yes. I made him return the money.'

'Without a struggle?'

'I threw a terrific scare into him. He hated to part with that money, but he didn't want to go to prison for blackmail.'

Mason said, 'You had given Boring ten thousand dollars in cash?'

'I had.'

'At what time?'

'At about five PM. He had stopped by my office just before closing time. He was there very briefly. I had the money ready for him.

'And from your office he went directly to the motel?'

'I believe he did. You should know. Apparently you were having him shadowed.'

'That's what the detective's report said,' Mason observed.

Winlock said, 'I am very deeply disturbed about this thing, Mr Mason. I cannot permit my wife to commit perjury simply in order to save our reputation. That's altogether too great a price.'

'And how do you know it's perjury?'

'Because Boring was in good health when I left him.'

'That's what you say,' Mason said, eyeing Winlock narrowly, 'but there's another explanation.'

'What?'

'That you killed him,' Mason said.

'*I* did!'

'That's right. That you went to Boring and threatened him with arrest, and Boring told you to go ahead and arrest and be damned; that you weren't going to push him around. You had an argument, hit him, inflicting fatal injuries, and removed the money you had given him as the result of his blackmail.

'In that event, your wife's testimony wouldn't be directed primarily at saving Dianne, but at saving you.

'The man was lying there dying when Dianne entered the motel unit. You were the last one to see him prior to the time Dianne saw him. The minute you state that he was alive and well when you saw him, you make yourself a murderer.'

'I can't help it,' Winlock said. 'I am going to tell the truth. I've steeped myself in deceit as much as I am going to.'

'Now then,' Mason went on, 'what would happen if your wife went on the stand and your stepson went on the stand and both of them swore positively that when *they* entered that unit in the motel they found Boring lying on his back, breathing heavily, with the odour of whisky overpoweringly strong?'

'If I were put on the stand I would still tell the truth.'

143

'Suppose you weren't put on the stand?'

Winlock got up and started pacing the floor, clenching and unclenching his hands. 'God help me,' he said, 'I don't know what I'd do. I'd probably get out of the country where I couldn't be interviewed. I—'

'You'd get out of the country,' Mason said, 'because you'd be avoiding a charge of murder.'

'Don't be foolish, Mr Mason. If I had killed him, I would be only too glad to ride along with the story my wife and stepson are thinking of concocting in order to purchase Dianne's silence. I would then perjure myself and swear that the man was unconscious and apparently drunk.'

Mason said, 'Unless this act you're now putting on is all a part of the overall scheme to save your own neck and to confuse me . . . The minute you tell me that this man was alive and well when you left, you put me in a position of suborning perjury in the event I permit your wife and stepson to testify as witnesses for the defence that he was lying there in a stupor, apparently dead drunk.'

'I can't help it, Mr Mason. I've gone just as far as I'm going to along the slimy path of deceit in this thing. I've got to a point now where I can't sleep, I can't live with myself.'

'And how does Mrs Winlock feel about all this?' Mason asked.

'Unfortunately, or fortunately, as the case may be, she doesn't share my feelings. Apparently the only thing that is bothering her is the question of how to prevent this situation from being disclosed, how to prevent her social set from knowing that she has been living a life of deceit for the past fourteen years, that she hasn't been married to me at all. Her only concern is for the immediate effect on her social and financial life.'

'All right,' Mason said, 'go home and talk it over with her. Remember this, as an attorney at law I'm obligated to do what is for the best interests of my client.

'*You* tell me that he was alive and well when you left, but your wife and your stepson tell me that he was lying there fatally injured; only, because his clothes were saturated with whisky, they thought he was drunk.

'I'm not in a position to take your word against theirs. I have to do what's for Dianne's best interests.'

Winlock said, 'You can't do it, Mason. You're a reputable attorney. You can't suborn perjury.'

'You think your wife is going to perjure herself?'

'I know it.'

'You don't think Boring might have been putting on an act for their benefit? That he had poured whisky over his clothes and was lying there, apparently in a stupor? That he then got up when you entered the unit and talked with you?'

'There was no odour of whisky on his garments when I talked with him.'

Mason said, 'If such is the case, *you* are Boring's murderer. You have to be.'

'Don't be a fool, Mason,' Winlock said.

'Under those circumstances,' Mason observed somewhat thoughtfully, 'the case would - under those circumstances – be mixed all to hell. Nobody would know what to do. It would shake this community to its foundations.'

'If my wife and my stepson get on the stand and commit perjury,' Winlock said, 'I suppose I have no alternative but to get on the stand and tell a similar story, but I'll tell you right now, Mason, it would be a lie.'

'Under those circumstances,' Mason said, '*I* wouldn't call *you* as a witness. But that doesn't keep me from calling Mrs Winlock and Marvin Harvey Palmer.'

Winlock looked at Mason, then hastily averted his eyes. 'I wish I knew the answer to this,' he said.

'And I wish *I* did,' Mason told him, eyeing him thoughtfully.

'I can, of course, get my wife out of the jurisdiction of the court,' Winlock said.

'Sure you can,' Mason said, 'but I'll warn you of one thing. If I decide to put on a defence and call your wife and stepson and they're not available, I'll tell the court the conversations I have had with them and the fact that they have offered to testify. I'll insist on having the case continued until they can be called as witnesses, and you can't stay out of the jurisdic-

145

tion of the court indefinitely. You have too many property interests here.'

Winlock shook his head, said, 'I have no alternative. I'm gripped in a vice.' He walked to the door, groped for the knob, and went out.

Della Street regarded Mason quizzically.

Five minutes later the telephone rang.

Della Street said, 'Mrs Winlock for you, Mr Mason.'

Mason took the receiver.

Again Mrs Winlock's voice, almost mockingly cool, said, 'Have you reached a decision yet, Mr Mason?'

'Not yet,' Mason said.

'I'll be available at my house, Mr Mason. Give me a few minutes to get ready. My son will be with me.'

'And you'll testify as you have indicated?' Mason asked.

'I'll testify as we have indicated, *provided* you will give me your word as a gentleman and an attorney that you and Dianne will preserve the secret of Dianne's relationship, and will accept the financial settlement offered by Mr Winlock.

'Good day, Mr Mason.'

Again the phone was hung up at the other end of the line.

At that minute two waiters appeared, bringing in the luncheon.

'Well, Mr Perry Mason,' Della Street said, when the waiters had left the room, 'you seem to have worked yourself into a major dilemma.'

Mason nodded, toyed with the food for a few minutes, then pushed his plate aside, got up, and started pacing the room.

'Know what you're going to do?' Della Street asked.

'Damn it!' Mason exploded. 'The evidence points to the fact that George Winlock is the murderer.'

'He has to be,' Della Street said. 'That is, unless Dianne is lying.'

'I have to take my client's story as the truth,' Mason said. 'I am bound to accept her statement at face value. And yet she has to be lying about making that phone call to the manager of the motel. Mrs Winlock must be the one who made that call. Dillard's testimony as to the time Dianne left clinches that.

146

Dianne simply didn't have time to get to the phone and make that call.

'Now then, the significant thing is that Mrs Winlock didn't make the call until *after* her husband had left the cabin *and* had a chance to report to her that he had frightened or forced Boring into returning the blackmail money.'

'Then that leaves George D. Winlock the murderer,' Della Street said.

'And he's handled things so cleverly,' Mason agreed, 'that if I do try to expose him as a murderer, I look like a heel. If, on the other hand, I put Mrs Winlock and her son on the stand and let them swear to the story they've offered to tell, I get Dianne off the hook but leave myself open to a charge of suborning perjury at any time Winlock wants to lower the boom on me.'

'Could this be a very shrewd, clever stunt that they jointly have carefully worked out and rehearsed?' Della Street asked.

'You're damn right it could,' Mason said.

'And,' she asked, 'what's going to be your counter-move?'

'I don't know,' Mason told her. 'At first I thought it was simply an offer to furnish perjured testimony and I was going to throw the whole thing out in the alley. Now I'm not so certain that it isn't a carefully, cunningly contrived plot to hamstring my defence and put me in such a position that I don't know what actually did happen.'

The lawyer resumed his pacing of the floor.

After a few minutes he said, 'Of course, Della, it's not up to me to prove who did murder the guy – that's up to the prosecution. My job is to prove Dianne innocent.'

'Can you do it?' she asked.

'With this testimony I could do it hands down,' Mason said.

Again the telephone rang.

'Paul Drake,' Della Street said.

'Hello, Perry,' Paul Drake said. 'I'm finished down here at the Restawhile Motel.'

'What did you find out?'

'The distance to be covered is about a hundred feet each way. Moving at a fairly normal rate of speed it takes about

147

thirty seconds each way. Moving at a rapid rate of speed, you cut that time down.

'Getting in, picking up the telephone, and putting the call through accounts for seven seconds. So her testimony is approximately correct. Figure about a minute and ten seconds as the outside time limit if she did what she said she did.'

"All right,' Mason said, 'here's something else for you, Paul. Drive down to the telephone booth three blocks down the street. Time yourself from the entrance of the motel. Call me from that booth and let me know how long it takes until you hear my voice. I'll be waiting here at the phone.'

'Okay,' Drake said, 'and then I want some lunch. I'm ravenous. I suppose you folks are sitting up there smug and well fed.'

'We're neither smug nor well fed,' Mason said. 'I'm sitting on the end of a great big limb and I'm not too certain somebody between me and the tree doesn't have a very sharp saw.

'Get busy and see what you can find out, Paul.'

Four minutes later, Paul Drake telephoned.

'Hello, Perry,' he said when he had the lawyer on the line. 'It took me exactly two minutes from the time I left the entrance of the motel to get down here, park my car, get in the telephone booth, close the door, dial you, and get your answer.'

'Hang it,' Mason said. 'Dianne could not have left the place and placed that call, or else the time element is all wrong.'

Drake said dryly, 'She was the last person to see Harrison Boring alive. You may be able to mix Dillard up on the time element but that's all it's going to amount to, just a technicality. The facts speak for themselves.'

'Of course,' Mason said into the telephone, almost musingly, 'the time Dianne left can be checked with physical facts. The time she entered is fixed only by Dillard's watch.

'Just suppose he made the mistake of setting his watch not by the radio but by the clock there in the motel office.'

'Would it help if you could show that?' Drake asked.

'Anything would help,' Mason said. 'That is, anything that clarifies the situation.'

'Or confuses it,' Drake said dryly. 'I'm going to get some lunch.'

Mason hung up the telephone, turned to Della Street. 'Two minutes,' he said.

'And that throws Dillard's time off about four minutes?'

'Something like that.'

Della Street said, 'He was looking at his watch in the dark and he *could* have misread the hands.'

'It's vital as far as Dianne is concerned,' Mason said.

'Of course,' she pointed out, 'it opens up some question of doubt, but after all she was in there at least ten minutes, even if Dillard did make a mistake.'

'She says she wasn't,' Mason said.

'But,' Della Street pointed out, 'she admits she remained long enough to search for and find the contract. She was only estimating the time.'

Mason said, 'The thing that annoys me is the smooth assurance of this district attorney, who acts on the assumption that this is just a simple routine matter of another preliminary hearing in another murder case and there's no reason on earth why he shouldn't have it all buttoned up inside of half a day.'

'But,' Della Street said, 'the *main* problem is whether Winlock is lying, whether the whole family isn't protecting the stepson, or who struck the fatal blow and when. After all, Dillard's time discrepancies are minor matters.'

Mason said, 'I have in my hand an opportunity to introduce testimony that will throw the district attorney's case out of the window, get Dianne in the clear, and at the same time get a property settlement for her running into a very substantial figure.

'If I do that, Winlock is either going to claim I was guilty of suborning perjury – or at least is in a position to do so any time he chooses to lower the boom.'

'What will happen if you *don't* do it?' Della Street asked.

'Then,' Mason said, 'Dianne is going to get bound over on a murder charge. She'll be in jail awaiting trial, she'll come up before a jury; by that time Mrs Winlock will have withdrawn her offer and sworn she never made it. It will be the word of Dianne against a lot of circumstantial evidence and against the evidence of a man who has a great deal of influence in the community, George D. Winlock.'

149

'Then I'll spring a dramatic surprise that Winlock is the girl's father and is testifying against her to protect himself. I'll make a high-pressure plea to the jury – and in all probability they'll convict Dianne of manslaughter rather than murder. That's about the best I can hope to accomplish. That's the price of trying to be ethical. To hell with it.'

Della Street, realizing the nature of the crisis which confronted the lawyer, watched him in worried silence.

CHAPTER 17

JUDGE TALENT said, 'This is the time heretofore fixed for resumption of the hearing in the case of the People of the State of California versus Dianne Alder. You were to let the Court know at this time whether you wish to put on a defence, Mr Mason.'

Mason said, 'If the Court please, this is not a simple matter. There are complications which I am not in a position to disclose but which nevertheless cause the defence some concern as to the best course to pursue.'

District Attorney Leland was on his feet. 'If the Court please, the defence has had all the time they asked for and I object to granting any further time.'

'I am not asking for further time,' Mason said, 'but I would like to clarify one matter in regard to the time element. I would like to ask a few more questions on cross-examination of the witness, Steven Dillard.'

'Is there any objection?' Judge Talent asked Leland.

'There is lots of objection, Your Honour. This man, Dillard, is actually a hostile witness. He is in the employ of defence counsel. He gave his testimony reluctantly and he gave it so that he shaded everything he could in favour of the defence. The cross-examination was completed, my case was closed, and I object to having counsel try these tactics of recalling a witness for further cross-examination. It's irregular.'

'The matter rests in the discretion of the Court,' Judge Talent said. 'Would you like to amplify your statement, Mr Mason?'

'I would, if the Court please. Dillard stated that the defendant was in the unit from nine o'clock to nine-twelve. Yet the records will show that the police were notified at nine-thirteen, which would indicate that the manager of the motel must have been in there at least by nine-twelve. The manager of the motel, in turn, was notified by some woman over the telephone that—'

'You don't need to go any further, Mr Mason. The Court is interested in the proper administration of justice. Your request will be granted. Mr Dillard, resume the stand, please.'

Dillard once more came to the stand.

Mason said, 'I would like to have you consult your notes in regard to the time element, Mr Dillard. I would ask the district attorney for the notes which you state you kept at the time.'

The district attorney grudgingly passed over the notebook.

Mason stood beside Dillard. 'These figures are scrawls, rather than figures,' he said. 'How do you explain that?'

'I was sitting there at the window and I took notes in the dark. I didn't want to turn on the light.'

'Now, you were also looking at your wrist watch in the dark in order to determine the time, were you not?'

'My wrist watch has luminous hands.'

'Is there any chance you could have missed the time by five minutes?'

'Certainly not. I could see the dial very clearly.'

'Could you have missed it by two minutes?'

'No.'

'By one minute?'

'Well, I'll put it this way, Mr Mason. I couldn't see the second hand, but I could see the hour hand and the minute hand and I might – I just might – have made a mistake of half or three-quarters of a minute; I don't think as much as a full minute.'

Mason said, 'If Dianne left that unit, got in her car, drove to a telephone, called the manager of the motel; if the manager of the motel had then gone down to the unit to look for herself and then returned and called the police, it is obvious that the police couldn't have received the call by nine-thirteen if Dianne had left the unit at nine-twelve.'

Dillard said nothing.

'Now, I notice that while the other figures are in the nature of scrawls,' Mason said, 'the words "blonde enters cabin" with the licence number of her automobile, TNM 148, and the hour 9.00, are written very neatly. And the words, "blonde leaves unit" with the figure 9.12 PM are also written very neatly. Can you explain that?'

'Well, I . . . I guess perhaps I had moved over to where the light was better.'

'Then,' Mason said, 'you didn't write those figures down *at the time* the defendant left the cabin. Perhaps you wrote them down later.'

'No, I wrote them at about that time.'

'At *about* that time, or at that time?'

'At that time.'

'Your Honour,' Leland said, 'this is no longer legitimate cross-examination. The question has been asked and answered, and counsel is now attempting to argue with the witness and browbeat him.'

Judge Talent said, 'There is rather a peculiar situation here. May I ask counsel if it is the contention of the defence that the defendant actually was the person who put through the telephone call to the manager of the motel, suggesting that there was something wrong with the occupant of Unit 10?'

Mason said, 'I feel that without jeopardizing the interests of the defendant, I can answer that question by saying that it may appear the call was made by her or by someone else and the time element may be the determining factor.'

'She couldn't have made that call,' Leland said. 'It had to have been someone else, and counsel is trying to take advantage of this peculiar situation in the time element to give his client a chance to claim she made the call.'

Mason, studying the notebook which had been kept by Dillard, apparently paid no attention to the objection.

'Mr Mason,' Judge Talent said, 'an objection has been made. Do you wish to argue it?'

'No, Your Honour.'

'I think the question has been asked and answered. I will sustain the objection.'

Mason turned to Dillard. 'All right, I'll ask you another question which has *not* been asked and answered, Mr Dillard. Isn't it a fact that you made this entry about the defendant entering the cabin with the licence number of her automobile, and putting down the time that she left the cabin, *before the defendant left the cabin*? And while you were sitting at a desk under a reading lamp where you could write these figures neatly and concisely?'

Dillard hesitated, then said, 'No.'

'And isn't it a further fact,' Mason said, 'that you are notoriously hot-tempered; that after the man with dark glasses left Unit 10, the decedent, Harrison T. Boring, who had caught you peeking through the parted curtain, came over to your unit, threatened you, and you lost your temper and hit him; that the blow knocked him down; that he hit his head on a stone and lay still; that you, realizing that you had seriously injured the man, picked him up, took him over to his own unit, opened the door, dropped him on the floor, poured whisky over him, returned to your unit and while you were debating what you were going to do next, saw the defendant enter the unit rented by Boring; that you thereupon quit watching the unit, debating what you were going to do to save your own skin, that while you were debating the matter you heard the defendant's car start and heard her drive off; that while you were still debating what to do, you heard the police arrive; that you at a time somewhat later wrote a synthetic record of the defendant's visit, approximating the time of her arrival and estimating the time of her departure, and then called your superior, Sid Nye, and asked that he come to your assistance?'

Leland got to his feet with a supercilious smile. 'Oh, Your Honour,' he said, 'this is altogether too absurd. This ...'

The district attorney suddenly broke off at the expression on the judge's face. Judge Talent was leaning forward from the bench, looking down at Moose Dillard.

The big man on the stand was clenching and unclenching his huge hands. His facial muscles were twisting in the manner of a grown man who wants to cry and has forgotten how.

Dillard wiped his forehead with the back of his hand.

'You'd better answer that question, Mr Dillard,' the judge said somewhat sternly, 'and answer it truthfully.'

'All right,' Dillard said. 'That's the way it happened. I clobbered the guy. Only, I didn't knock him down, he was standin' in the door of my unit calling me names and he made a pass at me. I beat him to the punch and clobbered him.

'The blow knocked him back and his head struck against the corner post on the porch and he slumped to the ground.

'I didn't know he'd been hurt too bad, but I'd been in enough trouble. I picked the guy up and carried him back to Unit 10 and dumped some whisky over him. Then I saw he was badly hurt. I went back and tried to figure what to do and I saw this girl come in.'

'The defendant?' Judge Talent asked.

'That's right. I didn't put down the time or anything. I went back over to the desk and sat there with my head in my hands. I heard her drive away and then after a while I heard the cops come and I knew I was in a spot.

'I called Sid Nye and told him "Hey Rube". He'd been in carnival life and I'd been in the circus. I knew that would get me reinforcements. I intended to tell him what had happened, but he brought Perry Mason down with him and then I knew I was in a real jam.

'Before they came, I faked that entry in the book. I just wanted to get the girl's visit down and didn't know what time she came or what time she left so I approximated it.

'Then I *did* want to get out of town. I didn't intend to do anything that would put this girl in a jam. I just wanted to save my own neck.'

Judge Talent looked at Leland.

The prosecutor stood for a moment, his facial expression indicating the confusion of his mind. Then he slowly seated himself as though his leg muscles had lost the strength to support him.

Judge Talent turned to Mason. 'Would you mind telling the Court how you deduced what happened, Mr Mason? Obviously it just occurred to you.'

Mason said, 'If the Court please, I had only to realize my client was telling the truth to appreciate the fact that something had to be wrong with the testimony of this witness. I then started searching for a possible explanation. When I saw the neat way the entry of Dianne's visit had been made, I knew it hadn't been written in the dark.

'When I saw the letters PM after the time, I knew the entry had been faked. No detective making notes on a night stake-out would write PM after the hour.

'I reproach myself for not seeing it sooner.'

'On the other hand,' Judge Talent said, 'the Court compliments you on a masterly cross-examination and on your quick thinking.'

The judge turned to the prosecutor.

'The case against the defendant is dismissed, and I think we had better take the witness, Dillard, into custody for perjury and a suspicion of homicide; although I have a feeling that he is probably telling the truth and the actual blow was struck in self-defence.

'Court's adjourned.'

CHAPTER 18

MASON, DELLA STREET, Paul Drake, and Dianne Alder sat in the bedroom of Mason's suite at the hotel.

Della Street said, 'I can't hold off the Press much longer, Chief. They're milling around there in the sitting-room and it's taking more than cocktails to hold them in line. They want information.'

Mason looked at Dianne. 'What do we do, Dianne?'

Dianne took a deep breath. 'As far as my father is concerned, he has repudiated me. I loved him at one time. I feel very fond of him now, but I recognize his weaknesses.

'As far as the woman who is living with him is concerned, she is a woman. She has problems of her own. She has built up a social position here and I don't want to sweep that out from under her.'

Again she took a deep breath, then smiled at Mason. 'I'm returning to Bolero Beach,' she said. 'I came up here as Dianne Alder, a model, and I'm going back to Bolero Beach as Dianne Alder.

'You can make whatever settlement you want to with my . . . my father.'

'You don't want to see him?'

She blinked back tears. 'He doesn't want to see me,' she said, 'and I can realize that it's dangerous for him to do so. I have no desire to wipe out the happiness of other people.'

Mason nodded to Della Street. 'That does it,' he said. 'We'll go out and give the reporters a statement.'

The undisputed 'Queen of Crime'

AGATHA CHRISTIE

Creator of Hercule Poirot and Miss Marple, two of the most famous sleuths in crime fiction. Weaver of perennially entertaining and ingenious tales of mystery and suspense with just that added twist that only she knows how to provide.

A SELECTION OF POPULAR READING IN PAN

Wilbur Smith
- [ ] WHEN THE LION FEEDS   30p (6/–)
Leslie Thomas
- [ ] THE VIRGIN SOLDIERS   25p (5/–)
- [ ] THE LOVE BEACH   30p (6/–)
Morris West
- [ ] THE SHOES OF THE FISHERMAN   25p (5/–)

NON-FICTION

Dr. Laurence J. Peter & Raymond Hull
- [ ] THE PETER PRINCIPLE   30p (6/–)
Sidney Smith
- [ ] 'WINGS' DAY   30p (6/–)
June Johns
- [ ] KING OF THE WITCHES (illus.)   25p (5/–)
Gavin Maxwell
- [ ] RAVEN SEEK THY BROTHER (illus.)   30p (6/–)
Dr. A. Ward Gardener & Dr. Peter J. Roylance
- [ ] NEW SAFETY AND FIRST-AID (illus.)   30p (6/–)
Vance Packard
- [ ] THE SEXUAL WILDERNESS   50p (10/–)
Leon Petulengro
- [ ] THE ROOTS OF HEALTH   20p (4/–)
Paul Davies
- [ ] THE FIELD OF WATERLOO (illus.)   25p (5/–)
'Adam Smith'
- [ ] THE MONEY GAME   25p (5/–)
Dr. Haim G. Ginott
- [ ] BETWEEN PARENT AND CHILD   25p (5/–)

Obtainable from all booksellers and newsagents. If you have any difficulty, please send purchase price plus 9d postage to P.O. Box 11, Falmouth, Cornwall. While every effort is made to keep prices low, it is sometimes necessary to increase prices at short notice. PAN Books reserve the right to show new retail prices on covers which may differ from the text or elsewhere.

I enclose a cheque/postal order for selected titles ticked above plus 9d a book to cover packing and postage.

NAME ....

ADDRESS ....

....